Trick or Treat on Murder

BONZAI
MOON

BonzaiMoon Books LLC
Houston, Texas
www.bonzaimoonbooks.com

1

Roland "Beanie" Bean stared at the email on his computer sent to him several minutes ago from Vivian Thomas-Bronson, his boss, the Managing Editor of the *Palmchat Gazette*, the award-winning newspaper where he worked as an investigative reporter.

Need Davenport story before end of day

Beanie typed a reply, letting Vivian know he'd completed the story and was sending it to her as an attachment. After receiving confirmation that his boss had received the article, he leaned back in the creaky leather chair behind his small desk in his tiny cubicle.

The Davenport story was a detailed timeline of events surrounding the sentencing trial of Belinda Davenport, a St. Killian socialite and boutique owner accused of murder. Several months ago, Belinda had been found guilty, but the punishment phase of her trial had wrapped up yesterday. A jury of Belinda's peers had decided she should spend the next fifteen years in prison.

Beanie had been in the courtroom when the sentence was handed down. His heart slamming, he'd kept his focus on Belinda, standing next to her team of high powered, high-priced lawyers. As the judge recited the number of years the mother of three would spend in prison, Beanie felt apprehensive. His testimony, among many others, including Belinda's husband, Bob—notably absent from the hearing—had been instrumental in securing Belinda's conviction. For one bizarre moment, Beanie imagined Belinda looking over her shoulder at him, giving him the evil eye, and mouthing that she would put him in the dirt for testifying against her.

He'd worried for nothing. Belinda showed no emotion when her fate was sealed. Just as she had been when the verdict in her murder trial was read, Belinda was expressionless.

Beanie dragged a hand down his face, thinking about the story: EASTER EGG HUNT KILLER GETS FIFTEEN YEARS. Despite being a crucial part of the narrative, Beanie hadn't wanted to write the story. Belinda Davenport had almost killed him, but Vivian believed his near demise made for great copy. She was probably right. The Easter egg hunt murder articles were still trending.

Nevertheless, Beanie thought the sentencing trial would be a good assignment for the *Palmchat Gazette's* new intern, Joshua Howard. A journalism major at the University of St. Killian, Joshua was smart, scrappy, always eager, and willing to help Beanie with anything he needed, no matter how menial or seemingly trivial. The kid reminded Beanie of himself. When he'd interned at the *Palmchat Gazette*, Beanie had been flexible, adaptable, and ambitious. He'd wanted to soak up as much real-life experience and knowledge about the newspaper business as he possibly could. From day one, two months ago, Joshua had been the same way.

Vivian had agreed to allow Joshua to shadow Beanie and write the article, with Beanie's supervision. The intern had been beyond excited for the opportunity.

Or so Beanie had thought.

Two days ago, on Monday, he and Joshua had discussed background details about the story. Over lunch at Beanie's favorite food truck in Pourciau Square—which also happened to be a fav of Joshua's—they brainstormed approaches and angles for the article. On Tuesday, he and Joshua planned to drive to the courthouse together, but the intern hadn't shown up to work. Beanie had called and texted several times to no avail. Beanie had finally given up and headed to the sentencing proceedings without the intern. Sitting in the courtroom gallery, Beanie continued to surreptitiously text the intern. Realizing Joshua had ghosted him, Beanie accessed his note-taking app to jot down details for the story. He couldn't believe Joshua had pulled a 'no-call, no-show.' The intern had always been dependable. Reliable. Despite having a second job at a local delivery company, Joshua had never missed his shift at the newspaper before.

Beanie sat forward. Actually, that wasn't right. Joshua had called in sick once. But the point was, he'd called Beanie to let him know he wouldn't be at work. Beanie glanced at the clock on his computer. Almost six o'clock. Wednesday was winding down. Once again, for the second day in a row, Joshua hadn't called or shown up at the *Palmchat Gazette.*

As a result, Beanie was forced to write the article on Belinda's sentencing because Joshua had flaked out on him. Beanie sighed. Didn't make sense that Joshua would blow off an assignment, especially a story he'd been stoked to write. Beanie hated to think he might have been wrong about the kid. He liked Joshua. The student was pleasant and attentive. Always in a good mood, but also serious about learning how to be a great reporter.

Though Joshua received assignments from all of the staff reporters, Beanie had taken the student under his wing, and thus, Joshua was referred to as "his intern." Unofficially, he'd been showing Joshua the ropes, guiding him, giving him pointers, and answering all of his questions. Beanie didn't mind being a mentor to a guy he'd bonded with, felt connected to, and genuinely liked.

Now Beanie worried he'd been wrong about the intern. He hoped the kid wasn't a flake. Joshua's interest in reporting for the *Palmchat Gazette* seemed real, and Beanie wanted to help him secure a permanent position. But maybe the kid wasn't really committed. Or was only pretending to be interested.

Turning to his computer, Beanie closed the files he'd been working on and powered down the machine.

If Joshua was having some personal problems that prevented him from working, then Beanie could understand. The intern just needed to be honest. But if the kid didn't want to be a reporter, then Beanie supposed that was fine, too. Again, he just wanted Joshua to be straight with him.

Determined to get answers, Beanie planned to call the intern.

But, contacting Joshua Howard was on his to-do list for tomorrow.

Making a note on his desk calendar, Beanie glanced at today's date. October 31. Halloween. The night for ghosts and goblins and all things scary and spooky. Grabbing his keys and phone, Beanie left his cubicle, thinking about the evening ahead, looking forward to taking his kids trick-or-treating.

"Daddy! Daddy!"

Beanie smiled at his boys, Ethan, and Evan, as they ran into the kitchen, squealing and laughing, dressed for an evening of tricks or treats. Four-year-old Ethan, who'd decided to be a Caribbean pirate, complete with an eyepatch and a fake sword, lunged at him. "En garde, daddy! Argh!"

Laughing, Beanie pretended to feint with his oldest son, dashing back and forth around the kitchen as Ethan chased him, demanding that Beanie walk the plank. The kid looked more like a cross between Captain Jack Sparrow and Captain Morgan than Blackbeard, but Beanie had to smile. The little swashbuckler was beyond cute. Evan, the two-year-old, was a little T-Rex, waddling around, giggling, and following his brother, mimicking Ethan.

"I surrender! I surrender!" said Beanie, chuckling. Dropping to his knees, he held his hands up. The boys converged on him with hugs that made Beanie's heart swell with indescribable love and joy. Kissing his boys' foreheads, Beanie pulled them closer to him, squeezing them tightly.

"You guys ready to go trick-or-treating?" asked Beanie, thinking about the wonderful memories he would make with his boys tonight.

"Yes!" the boys chorused in raucous delight. "Come on, daddy! Let's go! Come on!"

"Wait, wait, before you go ..." The melodic voice of Beanie's wife reached the kitchen before she did, dressed as, ironically, a mummy. Beanie smiled at his wife's costume, giving her a suggestive wink. The frayed straps of white fabric wound around her body couldn't hide her slim curves. Beanie couldn't wait to unwrap her, later when the boys were tuckered out and fast asleep and enjoy his very own Halloween treat.

"We have to get pictures!" said Noelle, returning the wink before turning her attention to the boys. "And some video!"

For the next ten minutes, Beanie and the boys created various poses, directed by Noelle, and then documented their excitement about trick-or-treating. After Noelle finally put the phone down, she gave the boys plastic child-sized pails decorated like orange pumpkins to collect candy. Then she dispensed behavioral instructions, sinking to her knees in front of the boys to admonish them about holding Beanie's hand at all times, and making sure they didn't run away from Beanie.

The boys nodded solemnly, but Beanie knew the kiddos were getting restless when Ethan said, "Okay, mommy, can we go now? They will run out of candy if we don't hurry!"

"Please, mommy, can we go?" pleaded little Evan, his lower lip trembling.

As she hugged the boys, Noelle glanced up at Beanie. The unshed tears in his wife's eyes nearly broke his heart. Noelle was overprotective, which was an understatement, and Beanie worked overtime to put her mind at ease and her fears to rest.

As his wife rose to her feet, she gave him a small smile.

Beanie told the boys to run to the door and wait for him. Alone with Noelle, Beanie grabbed his wife's hands and said, "It's gonna be okay, Elle. I promise, babe. We're going to be careful, and we're only trick-or-treating on our street with our neighbors that we know. And trust."

Nodding, Noelle pulled one hand from his to brush a strip of fabric from her face. Looking up at him, she said, "I know everything is going to be okay, and you're going to have a good time."

"Wish you could come with us," said Beanie, and he stole a quick kiss.

"Me, too," said Noelle. "But I have to stay here and pass out candy to everybody else's kids, and I'm totally fine with that, it's just ..."

"Just what?"

Noelle shook her head. "Nothing. It's silly."

"What's silly?" asked Beanie, sensing that something was troubling his wife. "Tell me."

"Something Old Wilson told me." Noelle exhaled. "He was talking about some wolf that people in the neighborhood have seen."

Beanie groaned inwardly. He wished Noelle wouldn't talk to "Old Wilson" as their neighbor Edward Wilson was known, but avoiding the nosy widower was impossible. The septuagenarian always had some wild, implausible story designed to cause unnecessary fear and worry.

Beanie sighed. "Babe, there's no wolf on this island."

"But Old Wilson said the wolf bit Mrs. Washington."

Shaking his head, Beanie said, "I doubt that."

Noelle said, "But—"

"Daddy, daddy!" Shouted Ethan and Evan as they ran back into the kitchen. "Come on! We want to trick or treat! Let's go!"

Beanie laughed, allowing the boys to push and pull him out of the kitchen, down the hall, and into the living room. Noelle followed them, repeating her safety instructions, which Beanie thought were unnecessary. Of course, he was going to make sure his little guys were safe. Part of Beanie was more than a little peeved that his wife felt the need to tell him how to take care of their kids, but he wasn't going to let her smothering ruin the evening.

He picked up Evan, grabbed Ethan's hand, and after a cursory kiss on his wife's cheek, he left the house, determined to make sure his boys had a great Halloween.

2

"Remember what Mommy said," Beanie called to the boys, who ran ahead of him along the wide sidewalk paved between the green manicured lawns of the modest single-family homes in Oyster Farms. Comprised of one-story bungalows painted pastel colors with white trim, the enclave was populated with a mix of white, blue, and pink-collar workers with a smattering of retirees.

"Don't run too far away from Daddy," instructed Beanie, though he wasn't worried about losing sight of his kids, or them running out into the street and getting hit by a car, or anything catastrophic. His little tykes were two of what looked like a hundred kids milling about, laughing, and squealing, and carefree. And there seemed to be just as many adults supervising and keeping an eye on the kiddos. Beanie felt secure that his boys were safe. He didn't need to hover.

Still, when he and the boys had walked out of the house, Beanie carried little Evan in his arms and held Ethan's hand. He'd known Noelle was watching. Worrying. After they'd visited the first three houses and had walked some distance from their corner house at the beginning of Dolphin Lane, Beanie had put Evan down and released Ethan's hand. Untethered and unrestrained, the boys alternated between running and skipping and hopping in front of him. Ethan, his little dervish, was wild and rowdy. Evan, the baby, waddled along, encumbered by his T-Rex costume, but giggling and squealing, determined to keep up with his brother. Now and then, the boys would turn and run back to him, commanding him to hurry, pulling him along to the next house.

Hands in the pockets of his jeans, Beanie smiled to himself as Ethan brandished his sword at the other kids he and his little brother came in contact with, challenging them to "en garde," laughing with his neighborhood friends.

Dozens of other families were out, enjoying the balmy atmosphere and the cool, salty ocean breeze. Those who didn't have little ones were giving out candy, standing on their porches, dispensing sweets. It was a nice night for trick-or-treating.

Strolling along, Beanie reflected on the neighborhood. The three-bedroom house he shared with Noelle was nicer than the two-bedroom house where he and his twin sister Robyn had grown up. Their Dolphin Lane bungalow had been newly constructed by a home builder who'd purchased a large tract of untamed jungle. Unofficially, it was referred to as "new Oyster Farms," but Beanie didn't think it merited the designation just because the houses had been built twenty years after the original track houses were built.

At one time, Beanie had contemplated leaving Oyster Farms. Not that he and Noelle had the finances to pull up stakes. But he'd dreamed of one day making a residential upgrade. Beanie hoped to write a true-crime book detailing a high-profile case he'd covered about an engineer who'd been decapitated. Noelle was thinking of teaching full-time at the university. Career advancement would bring the money they needed to move on up.

Montmarch, the enclave of the superrich and one percent, was out of the question—unless they won the lottery. Avalon Estates had once been on his list. But not anymore.

When he'd discovered a dead body at an Avalon Estates mansion during an Easter egg hunt earlier that year, Beanie had changed his mind about the luxurious neighborhood. The exclusive suburb was worse than Peyton Place. Too many secrets and lies.

For now, he and his family would stay put in Oyster Farms.

Minutes later, Beanie herded the boys up the flagstone path to the front porch of Old Wilson, dressed like Gandalf the Gray from the Lord of the Rings. Standing behind a large barrel of candy, the man known as the most prolific gossip in the neighborhood encouraged the kids to take as much candy as they desired. Naturally, Ethan used both hands to fill his pail, laughing and jostling with other neighborhood boys his age. Beanie lifted Evan in the air and picked out a few pieces for the little one.

"No, let me do it, Daddy!" Protested Evan, squirming in Beanie's arms.

Laughing, Old Wilson said, "How about I hold your pail while your daddy holds you over the barrel and you can dig in?"

Evan clapped his hands, obviously excited by Old Wilson's idea, which Beanie appreciated. Carefully holding his youngest over the barrel, Beanie laughed as Evan's little fingers grasped the candy.

"I've been meaning to ask you," said Old Wilson, his voice lowered beneath the squeals and laughter of the children converged around the barrel.

"What's that?" asked Beanie as Evan plunged his hands into the sea of plastic-wrapped candy pieces.

"You heard about the wolf, right?" asked Old Wilson, whispering the words from the side of his mouth.

Beanie suppressed an annoyed exhale as he moved Evan away from the barrel, ignoring the little guy's protests, and put him on the ground.

"Is it really a wolf?" asked Beanie.

"Daddy, I want to get candy!" said Evan, pulling on Beanie's jeans.

"Oh, for sure, it's a wolf," said Old Wilson.

Taking Evan's pail of candy from Old Wilson, Beanie crouched in front of his son and gave it to him. "Here's your candy, little man."

"Thank you, Daddy!" Evan smiled.

Rising to his feet, Beanie asked Old Wilson, "Did you see the wolf?"

"Didn't have to see it," said Old Wilson. "Heard about what it did. Attacked Mrs. Washington. Lunged at her and bit her wrist while she was walking her cat the other night."

"Walking her cat?" asked Beanie, even more skeptical of the story.

Nodding, Old Wilson said, "And Mr. Turner, the jitney driver, had just gotten off work and was going into his house when the wolf got ahold of him. Took a chunk out of his leg. Had to get fifteen stitches."

"C'mon, Daddy, let's go!" demanded Ethan, grabbing the tail of Beanie's T-shirt.

Knowing that Ethan wanted to keep up with his friends, most of whom had already moved on to other houses, Beanie nodded at Old Wilson and thanked him for the candy.

"Might be something you should write about in the paper," called out Old Wilson as Beanie scooped up Evan and grabbed Ethan's hand. "Folks need to know to be careful, especially at night."

As Beanie walked away, he shook his head at Old Wilson. The injuries to Mrs. Washington and Mr. Turner were concerning, but Beanie wasn't convinced a wolf was the culprit. More likely, it was a large dog. Probably a German Shepherd. At night, that breed of dog might be mistaken for a wolf.

After handfuls of candy from the next three houses, Beanie and the boys approached the doorway of Dr. Walter Zeller. A retired psychiatrist, Zeller was pleasant, polite, and quick to dispense unwanted parenting advice. Despite having no children of his own, the man had a knack for telling you how you were raising your kids wrong. Beanie tried to ignore the man's two cents, but Zeller had spent years getting into people's heads and presented himself as a credible authority. A slight hesitation or a frown from Zeller could make Beanie question his parenting skills. According to Zeller, too much discipline and negative reinforcement and insufficient structure and guidance might be the difference between a philanthropist and a psychopath.

Though he wasn't in the mood for Dr. Zeller's latest opinion, Beanie followed the boys up the pathway leading to the porch. Moments later, Dr. Zeller engaged the boys in conversation, making them laugh as he dropped candy into their pails.

"Looks like you little gentlemen have quite a haul," remarked Dr. Zeller, smiling at Ethan and Evan.

"We got lots of candy!" exclaimed Ethan. "We have candy for a long, long time!"

"Lots of candy!" echoed Evan.

"Maybe too much candy," said Beanie, wondering if Dr. Zeller disapproved of how permissive he'd been with the sweets.

As Ethan protested, Dr. Zeller laughed and said, "Well, if there's a time for too much candy, it's definitely Halloween."

Nodding, Beanie said, "Guys, tell Dr. Zeller, 'thank you.'"

"Thank you, Dr. Zeller!" chorused the boys.

"Where are you off to next?" asked Dr. Zeller.

"We're off to get more candy!" shouted Ethan as he turned and skipped down the pathway.

"More candy!" said Evan, waddling behind his brother.

"Guys, wait up," Beanie called to the boys.

"Before you go …" said Dr. Zeller.

Beanie cringed, trying to prepare himself for the parenting tips he hadn't requested.

"You might want to avoid the Volkov house," said Dr. Zeller, apprehension in his dark eyes.

"The Volkov house?" Beanie frowned. "Why?"

"Well, you know, they just moved to the neighborhood," said Dr. Zeller, glancing away. "They might not be giving out Halloween candy. I wouldn't want your boys to be disappointed."

Shrugging, Beanie said, "Well, we'll just check anyway, and if they're not, then—"

"I really think you should stay away from that house," said Dr. Zeller. "Don't take your boys there."

Before Beanie could ask the retiree to explain exactly what he meant, Dr. Zeller retreated into his small bungalow and closed the door behind him.

"Daddy! Come on! Let's go!" shouted Ethan.

Turning from the door, Beanie jogged down the porch steps and hurried to his kids. Resolved to put Dr. Zeller's strange warning out of his mind, Beanie figured the retiree was taking the spooky, Halloween spirit a little too far.

Leaving the retired psychiatrist's house, Beanie and the boys strolled toward the cul-de-sac, stopping at four more houses. The next stop was the home of Mr. Mendez, who'd moved to the neighborhood three years ago. The George Hamilton lookalike was a confirmed bachelor with lots of lady friends, one of whom stood next to him. Arguably twenty years younger than Mendez, the buxom blonde was dressed as a Playboy Bunny as she doled out candy. Beanie didn't mind the risqué outfit, but he knew Noelle would be pissed, so he didn't plan to tell her. Mr. Mendez was dressed as Hugh Hefner, complete with velvet smoking jacket, a fake cigar, and a smug, smarmy smile. Their costumes were ridiculously inappropriate for a neighborhood of families, widows, and retirees.

Mr. Mendez waved at Beanie. After returning the greeting, Beanie glanced at his watch. Almost a quarter to nine. Beanie thought it might be time to head home when he caught snatches of the conversation between a group of teenagers huddled behind him on the street.

"I bet you fools won't go to Mason's house," said one of the boys, cackling with laughter.

"I ain't trying to get killed and cut up!"

"That's what he did to his wife," said another, chuckling, though his voice held notes of wariness.

"And then he buried the body parts under that mango tree in his backyard!"

The boys erupted into laughter as they lumbered down the street, hooting and calling to other friends.

Beanie turned his head, staring at the rowdy group, disappointed and disturbed by their unabashed glee at the demise and dismemberment of another human being. But he couldn't throw stones. He'd been a teenager once, full of piss and vinegar, laughing inappropriately at inopportune moments. And in a few years, his boys would be part of a group of rowdy youths. Beanie shuddered at the thought. He wasn't ready for the boys to be teens, rebellious one moment, and sullen the next. He was content to enjoy his kids as they were right now.

The "Mason" the teens had been laughing about was Rufus Mason, the old man who lived in the center of the cul-de-sac. Beanie remembered being a kid when he'd first heard the rumors about the former science teacher murdering his wife. He wasn't sure how the stories had started, but they stemmed from the fact that Mason's wife, Daisy, disappeared without explanation. Mason never filed a missing person report. He'd gone on with his life as though his wife's absence wasn't strange or suspicious. Whenever he was asked about his wife, Mason would mumble a cryptic comment about the woman being long gone and unlikely to return.

Beanie wasn't sure he believed the rumors, but it wasn't hard for neighbors to assume the worse. Mason hardly left his house, and when he did, the tall, pallid man—a dead ringer for Lurch, the character from the Addams Family—never spoke to anyone. Granted, the man looked like a ghoul and was socially awkward, but that didn't mean he deserved to be branded as a killer.

When the boys came back, Beanie crouched down and said, "Guys, I think we need to head on home."

"No, Daddy, no!" Ethan and Evan chorused their protest with quivering lower lips.

Ethan said, "Please, can we go to just one more house?"

"Please, Daddy!" said Evan, near tears as he rushed into Beanie's arms and gazed up at him.

Unable to resist his boys' blatant emotional blackmail, Beanie conceded to visiting one more neighbor.

"We don't want to get in trouble with Mommy," Beanie warned as they strolled along the circle. He suspected Noelle was already upset that they hadn't returned at eight o'clock. His wife hadn't given them a curfew, but the boys were usually bathed and tucked into bed by eight-thirty. Halloween had fallen on a weeknight. Ethan had preschool in the morning while Evan would be taken to Noelle's mom's house before attending an early childhood development center.

The boys were already off schedule and might be cranky and sluggish in the morning, but Beanie didn't mind. Sharing these moments with his boys, making memories that would last a lifetime, was more important to him than well-rested, obedient kids.

"Let's go to this house, Daddy!" said Ethan, taking off across the manicured lawn of a peach-colored bungalow. Evan followed his brother, laughing and squealing as he joined Ethan on the wide porch.

Beanie frowned as his son ran toward the house Dr. Zeller had warned them to avoid—the Volkov house, occupied by Ivan and Natalya, a young

Russian couple who'd moved to the neighborhood a year ago. Ivan Volkov was a pharmaceutical salesman, according to Old Wilson, and his wife worked from home. Old Wilson hadn't been able to determine exactly what kind of work Natalya did, but Beanie was sure the old man wouldn't rest until he found out.

As Beanie walked up the pathway toward the porch, he smiled at Mrs. Dishman, and her three girls, all of them dressed as Disney princesses, who were leaving the Volkov's place. At the door, Ethan and Evan were holding their pails up, receiving several pieces of candy.

After waving to the salesman, who barely nodded and gave him a perfunctory smile, Beanie regarded the lanky, pale man. His shoulders hunched, he seemed tense and furtive, eyes darting back and forth. His hand shook as he dropped candy into Ethan's pail. Beanie wondered if something was wrong with the guy. Or, was he putting on an act for Halloween?

Dr. Zeller's warning whispered through Beanie's mind. Had the former psychiatrist been trying to tell him that Volkov was weird? Or slightly off? Or maybe…? Beanie wasn't sure what Dr. Zeller's warning was about. Maybe Zeller had talked to Volkov and detected some underlying psychosis. Some mental issue that might scare children.

Ethan and Evan thanked the salesman, then turned and headed back toward Beanie, who was starting to think that maybe the guy was—

Evan let out a high-pitched scream, dropped his pail of candy, and ran toward Beanie. "Daddy! Daddy!"

His heart exploding with panic, Beanie picked up Evan as Ethan shouted in terror and scrambled between Beanie's legs. What was that—

Deep guttural barking sent trepidation racing through Beanie's veins. More horrifying screams split the air, followed by shouting and yelling, warnings to get back and stay away.

Confused, Beanie turned.

A huge Siberian husky charged toward the porch, barreling toward Beanie and his boys, growling. The dog's ice-blue eyes seemed to glow as the animal bared its teeth and lunged. Determined to protect his boys, with his own life, if it came to that, Beanie scooped up Ethan and told both boys to hold on tight to him.

"No! Stop!" screamed Volkov, running toward the dog, stepping in front of the beast, blocking its attack. "STOP!"

The husky halted, stared up at Volkov, and then sat on the lawn.

Volkov spoke to the dog in Russian, admonishing the animal, pointing his finger at the husky as though the dog was a recalcitrant, disobedient child.

His panic subsiding, Beanie put the boys down but continued to hold their hands as Volkov pointed toward the door, continuing to fuss at the dog. Rising on all fours, its head hanging, the dog whimpered as it walked toward the door, followed by Volkov.

As relief flooded Beanie, he exhaled and crouched down between his boys. "You guys okay?"

"Mean doggie, Daddy," said Evan, frowning, a hint of righteous anger in his tremulous tone. "Bad doggie!"

"It's okay, buddy," said Beanie, kissing Evan's forehead. "Daddy wasn't going to let the mean dog hurt you."

"I wasn't scared, Daddy," said Ethan, though his wild, wide-eyed stare proved otherwise. "I have my sword to protect you!"

Beanie let out a nervous chuckle. "Okay, guys, let's find your candy."

For the next ten minutes, Beanie and the boys, along with the help of a few other neighbors and their kids, searched the lawn for the candy the boys had dropped when the husky lunged at them.

"I am sorry about dog," said a voice behind Beanie.

Beanie faced Ivan Volkov. "Maybe you should keep him on a leash."

"She," said Volkov, his gaze contrite, but still furtive.

Beanie frowned. "What?"

"The dog," said Volkov. "It is female."

"Regardless," said Beanie, pissed that the man thought it necessary to point out the dog's sex, as though that would have mattered if the dog had attacked the boys. "This neighborhood does have leash laws."

"I am aware," said Volkov. "However, it was not my intention for dog to get out, but she is very crafty girl. She is to stay in house but—"

The door opened, and a woman rushed out of the house. Her face flushed, she seemed out of breath as she hurried over to Beanie and Volkov. Turning to the woman, Volkov spoke harshly to her in Russian—the same manner in which he'd spoken to the husky. She glared at him, but stayed quiet, shaking her head and hugging her thin arms around her bony torso, which was clad in baggy clothes that hung from her frame.

With an angry exhale, Ivan Volkov faced Beanie and introduced the woman as his wife, Natalya.

When Beanie shook her hand, it was strong and heavy. As her fingers grasped his painfully, Beanie caught a pungent whiff of cloves and pepper.

"Nice to meet you," said Beanie, and as he pulled his hand from her death grip, he stared at her eyes. The ice blue irises, glowing in the fading sunlight, sent an odd chill through him.

"Please forgive dog," said the woman, wringing her hands as she stared at Beanie. "She is usually not aggressive. She has trouble with new environment. New surroundings. Please, do not be upset."

"I would not let her hurt children," said Volkov, slipping an arm around his splotchy-faced wife.

Still disturbed by the woman's strange eyes, Beanie said, "There are a lot of young kids and older people with limited mobility in this neighborhood, so I hope you'll make every effort to keep the dog from getting out."

3

"Mommy, a wolf tried to eat us!" exclaimed two-year-old Evan as Beanie handed him to Noelle.

"It came running at us, Mommy," said Ethan, whirling around the kitchen, thrusting and parrying at invisible opponents with his cardboard cutlass. "But I wasn't afraid of that crazy wolf! I had my sword, and I was going to cut his head off!"

Beanie groaned inwardly as Noelle glared at him. He'd known the boys wouldn't be able to keep the Siberian husky pseudo attack to themselves. After refilling their pails with the candy they'd accidentally dropped, the boys had chattered on and on about the husky, which they were convinced was a wolf despite Beanie's attempts to correct them. As they'd walked home, Beanie had tried to think of how he would explain the incident to Noelle. What words and phrases could he employ to convince her that the situation wasn't as dire as the boys would make it out to be? Beanie couldn't think of anything.

Standing in the kitchen, staring at his wife, who stared at him with the fierce anger of a proud lioness, Beanie knew he was in trouble. Might as well just take his punishment.

"It wasn't a wolf," Beanie told his wife, though he doubted it matter to her. The fact that anything had threatened her kids was, in Noelle's view, beyond horrible. The fact that Beanie had allowed something to threaten her kids was, in Noelle's view, a fate worse than death. Beanie's death.

Rolling her eyes, Noelle held Evan close, kissing his face and whispering soothing words against his forehead. "It's okay, sweetheart. Mommy's here."

Beanie resisted the urge to roll his eyes. He didn't like Noelle's tone when she'd said, Mommy's here. It was like she was telling Evan things would be okay because Mommy was there, but Daddy hadn't been. Daddy had almost let a wolf eat them, but Mommy would make everything alright. Beanie knew that was what Noelle was thinking, but she was wrong.

Daddy had been there for his boys. He would always be there for Evan and Ethan. Everything he did was for his boys to be safe and happy and healthy, so they could have the best life he could give them. When that husky had charged them, all Beanie could think was that he would give his life to save his boys. He'd been prepared to throw the boys to the ground and cover them with his body. He'd been willing to let the dog bite a chunk out of his backside to keep the beast away from his kids.

"It was a dog," said Beanie, taking a seat at the table. "Not a wolf."

Sighing, Noelle joined him at the table, maneuvering Evan onto her lap. "Are you sure?"

"Elle, I was there, okay," said Beanie. "I saw it when it came running at us—"

"So, the wolf did attack you?" demanded Noelle, a blatant accusation in her tone.

"It was not a wolf," said Beanie through gritted teeth. "It was a Siberian husky. You know how they look? Like wolves. But I saw it, and it was a dog. A huge dog, but definitely a dog. Not a wolf."

"Mommy!" Ethan ran to Noelle and wrapped his arms around her. "Can we have candy now?"

"Candy, Mommy, candy!" said Evan, wriggling in Noelle's arms.

"Bath first," said Noelle.

"Nooooooo!" protested Ethan, dropping to the floor, stomping his feet, and pounding his fists against the tile. "No bath, candy!"

"Candy!" agreed Evan, squirming, anxious to join his brother on the floor.

Ethan jumped to his feet and lunged at Beanie, vaulting into his lap.

"Whoa!" said Beanie, laughing as he circled his arms around the energetic little guy, struggling to hold onto his oldest son. "Give Daddy a little warning the next time."

Gazing at him imploringly, Ethan said, "Can we have candy, Daddy? Please?"

Beanie glanced at Noelle.

His wife smiled and shook her head at Ethan's attempt to pit his parents against each other.

"You can have candy," said Beanie, tweaking Ethan's little nose.

"Yay!" cheered Ethan. "Candy!"

"Candy!" echoed Evan, clapping his little hands.

"After you take your bath," said Beanie, laughing at Ethan's sour expression.

"Aw, Daddy," complained Ethan, his lower lip poked out as he slid from Beanie's lap.

"Come on," said Noelle, standing. Moving Evan to her other hip, she held out a hand for Ethan. "The quicker you guys take your bath, the quicker you can have one piece of candy."

"Aw, Mommy, just one?" asked Ethan, grabbing Noelle's hand. "Can't we have two pieces? We were good. We held Daddy's hand like you told us."

"Ha!" said Beanie, marveling at the little guy's selective memory.

Walking out of the kitchen, Ethan glanced over his shoulder and put a finger to his lips, signaling to Beanie to go along with the ruse.

Beanie gave Ethan a thumbs up and chuckled to himself. As his wife and kids left the kitchen, Ethan was still negotiating with Noelle about how many pieces of candy he could have before bedtime. Beanie was certain that Noelle preferred they had no candy tonight. Beanie agreed. Sugar at nine o'clock at night would have the boys riled up and bouncing off the walls. There was no telling how long it would take them to crash.

Maybe they could give the boys hot chocolate instead. With whipped crème. The little tykes would riot and insist that it wasn't fair, but the warm milk would put them to sleep. It was already half an hour past their bedtime.

Rising from his chair, Beanie walked to the panty. As he searched for the box of instant hot chocolate powder, his thoughts shifted to the Siberian husky. Maybe Zeller had been trying to warn him about the dog? That huge dog with the ice-blue glowing eyes had to be the "wolf" terrorizing the neighborhood. The husky had those lupine features people associated with wolves. Recalling the beast's bared teeth, Beanie was sure the dog could separate a finger from its hand with one quick chomp.

Locating the box of hot chocolate, Beanie shuddered, thinking of the animal's ferociousness. The dog had come at them like a hound out of hades. The husky had been out for blood. He would probably be in the emergency room right now, if not for Ivan Volkov.

Beanie grabbed some mugs from an overhead cabinet. Anger engulfed him. The Volkovs should not have allowed an aggressive dog to roam without a leash. It was beyond irresponsible. It was dangerous. Beanie didn't accept their half-hearted apologies. They'd insisted that the dog was harmless, but Beanie didn't buy it. Those ice-blue eyes had been cold-blooded.

A strange, odd chill passed through Beanie. A familiar chill. The same chill he'd felt when he'd stared into the eyes of Natalya Volkov.

"Hey ..."

Beanie turned. Noelle leaned against the entryway into the kitchen, giving him a small smile.

"Where are the boys?" Beanie walked to the table and put the mugs down.

"You're not going to believe this," said Noelle. "They're asleep."

Gaping, Beanie said, "Asleep? I thought they wanted candy."

Noelle strolled to the table and pulled out a chair. "So did I, but I guess all the trick-or-treating tuckered them out. And maybe the warm bath had something to do with it. They were exhausted, so I promised them a piece of candy for breakfast."

"Candy for breakfast?" Beanie chuckled. "Elle, you know the boys are going to hold you to that."

"Maybe they'll forget I said it," said Noelle, shrugging.

"And maybe they won't," said Beanie.

Noelle bit her bottom lip. "Hmmm. You're probably right. So, maybe we should find some candy that won't spoil their appetites for the rest of the day."

"Good idea," said Beanie. "I'll get their candy pails."

Ten minutes later, Beanie and Noelle sat at the table, examining the candy the boys had received, piece by piece.

"This is a lot of candy," said Noelle, holding up yet another foil-wrapped Hershey's kiss. "Maybe too much. They don't need all this junk."

"And we don't need outrageous dentist bills," grumbled Beanie.

"I think we should pick out five pieces for each of them," said Noelle. "And then the rest of the candy we can split and take to work and make our co-workers eat it."

Beanie shrugged. "Sounds good."

Nodding, Noelle took out a few more pieces of candy and scrutinized the shiny wrappers. "By the way …"

Waiting for his wife to speak, Beanie pulled out a peppermint and added it to the pile of sweets he'd designated as candy he would consider allowing Ethan to have.

"During their bath, all the boys could talk about was how brave Daddy was," said Noelle, peering intently at a package of gummy bears. "And how Daddy protected them and wouldn't let the mean wolf eat them."

Beanie stared at Noelle, smiling.

"So, I owe you an apology," said Noelle.

"For what?" asked Beanie, though he knew, and he adored his wife for her sensitive thoughtfulness.

"When the boys said the wolf tried to eat them—"

"It was a dog," corrected Beanie, putting a small package of licorice in the pile he was taking to the *Palmchat Gazette*. He knew Ethan wasn't a fan of the bitter candy.

"Wolf. Dog. Whatever," said Noelle. "I was upset that the dog tried to attack you and the boys."

"So was I," said Beanie.

Noelle sighed. "It made me regret agreeing to let the boys trick-or-treat because I was so afraid that something horrible was going to happen and it did, and I thought—"

"You thought that you couldn't trust your kid's father to take care of his own kids?"

Giving him a sassy look, Noelle said, "I'm trying to tell you that I'm sorry for being a hovering, helicopter mom."

"It's okay, babe," said Beanie, leaning over to kiss her cheek. "I know you mean well."

"I don't know where the tendencies come from," said Noelle. "I wasn't raised with an overprotective mother. She loved me, but Mom was out doing her own thing quite often, which gave me the opportunity to make some of the worse decisions of my life."

Noelle looked down and busied herself with examining candy.

Beanie knew what his wife considered the worst decision of her life. Joining the PC-5 island cartel when she was a teenager was a mistake his wife had rectified but still regularly beat herself up about. Beanie wished his wife would focus more on everything she'd accomplished than her regrets. She'd escaped the gang, got a degree from a prestigious university in the States, and was a well-respected pharmacist. She was a wonderful mother and a dedicated wife. She had more than made up for her youthful indiscretions.

"You know, babe," began Beanie, hoping to pivot the conversation to the reason for Noelle's overprotectiveness. "I think that because you had little supervision, you think that led to bad decisions, so maybe you feel the boys won't make bad choices if you're hyper-vigilant."

"Hyper-vigilant?" Noelle scoffed. "Seriously? I'm a mother who fiercely loves her children, so that makes me hyper-vigilant?"

Beanie plucked a pixie stix from Ethan's pail and twirled it between his fingers. "Okay, maybe hyper-vigilant isn't the right word."

"What's the right word?"

"Hmmm ..." said Beanie, hesitating. Honestly, his wife could be a "smother" at times, but he decided to keep that opinion to himself because he enjoyed relations with his wife and didn't want to piss her off or put her in the mood to deny him.

"Roland?" prompted Noelle, staring at him.

"You have a passionate dedication to your children," said Beanie. "And I love you for that and so many other reasons."

Noelle rolled her eyes and then added a wry smile. "Whatever. You know you think I'm a smother."

"Smother?" exclaimed Beanie, with mock surprise. "What? No! You? A smother? I would never think that."

"Yeah, right," said Noelle, laughing. "Let's just finish this candy. Speaking of which, are you having a hard time finding some decent pieces?"

Beanie chuckled. "There is a lot of bad candy in these pails."

"Some of it's old," said Noelle, shaking her head. "And some of it is not even candy. I keep finding pecans."

"I came across a few pencils," said Beanie.

"There were some Bible Scriptures on folded pieces of paper," said Noelle. "Admonishing the children to honor their parents."

"Probably from Mrs. McMorris," said Beanie, thinking of the church secretary as he continued rummaging through Ethan's pail. "And then I found a—"

Noelle screamed, jumped up, and scurried to the opposite side of the kitchen.

"Babe, what is it?" asked Beanie, staring at his wife's wild, horrified stare. She'd probably seen a spider, or maybe a lizard. He wouldn't put it past Ethan to have caught one and slipped it into his pail.

"In the pail ..." whispered Noelle, trembling as she pointed toward the table.

Standing, Beanie walked to his wife and took her hands. "What did you see?"

Swallowing, Noelle closed her eyes and shook her head.

Beanie sighed and returned to the table. Approaching Evan's pail cautiously, he walked slowly, his heartbeat increasing as he leaned over the pail.

"What the ..." whispered Beanie, understanding why Noelle was spooked.

Nestled in the middle of the candy was a human finger.

4

"Gross!" exclaimed Sophie Carter. "Are you serious? You found an actual human finger in the Halloween candy?"

Stevie Bishop looked skeptical. "Are you sure it wasn't a piece of candy shaped like a human finger?"

Regarding his fellow *Palmchat Gazette* reporters, who were crowded around his desk, Beanie said, "It was a human finger."

After arriving at the newspaper's office in downtown St. Killian, Beanie had made himself a cup of coffee and then beckoned his co-workers to his small cubicle. For the past hour, instead of working, he'd recounted the strange, stomach-churning incident that had occurred in his kitchen last night.

"That's a shame!" complained Caleb Olivier, the most senior reporter. "People are so crazy and evil these days. Folks just didn't do that kind of sick crap when I was a kid. You could enjoy Halloween without worrying that somebody would put severed body parts in your candy bag!"

"The boys didn't see the finger, did they?" asked Sophie, her expression stricken.

"No, no, thank God, they were asleep," said Beanie, taking another sip of coffee. "Last thing Evan needed was to see a severed finger. Little guy already saw a dead body."

"But he didn't know what it was," said Stevie.

Beanie exhaled. "I know, but Noelle would have been pissed if those boys had seen the finger. She was already leery about them trick-or-treating because of the wolf."

"What wolf?" asked Stevie.

Beanie told them about Old Wilson's unfounded allegations about the wolf.

"So, a wolf is terrorizing Oyster Farms?" asked Sophie, her eyes alight with prurient interest.

"Ain't no danged wolf," said Caleb. "Weren't you listening? He said it was a dog. One of them Russian dogs."

"A Siberian husky," clarified Beanie. "It tried to attack us, but the owner was there to stop it. Anyway, Noelle was already upset about that, and then she finds a finger, so … I'm quite sure the boys will never trick-or-treat again."

"How's your wife doing?" asked Caleb.

Beanie ran a hand down the back of his neck. "She was horrified at first, but after the cops showed up and got the finger out of the house, she calmed down."

Sophie shook her head. "Can't believe one of your neighbors was passing out body parts for Halloween."

"Talk about taking Halloween to the extreme," said Stevie.

"I don't think anyone was passing out body parts," said Beanie, alarmed by the idea. "As far as I know, no other kids got a gruesome surprise, and trust me, I would know because my nosy neighbors would have told me."

Stevie cocked his head. "So you think … wait, what do you think? How did the finger get in the candy pail?"

"Somebody put it in there," said Caleb. "One of his crazy neighbors."

Caleb's mention of a crazy neighbor made Beanie think of Rufus Mason, but he dismissed the thought and said, "Actually, I think the husky bit someone's finger off and dropped it on the grass when it lunged at us and then when we were picking up the candy the boys dropped, we accidentally put the finger in the pail."

Sophie frowned. "Don't you think you would have realized it if you'd picked up a finger?"

"Yeah, I would have," conceded Beanie. "But little Evan might not have known."

Scoffing, Caleb folded his arms across his chest. "I still think it was one of your neighbors."

Nodding, Stevie agreed. "Don't you live close to that crazy old dude who killed his wife and cut her up?"

"Rufus Mason," said Caleb, nodding. "I covered that case. The wife just up and went missing."

"Maybe he's at it again," suggested Sophie.

Beanie shook his head. "I doubt it." He didn't like the idea of living several doors down from a deranged man who liked to dismember people and bury them in his backyard.

Caleb mused, "Wonder who the finger belongs to …"

Anxious to change the subject, Beanie said, "Speaking of wondering about things … have you guys seen or heard from Joshua?"

Shrugging, Sophie shook her head. "Nope."

Stevie said, "Don't think so."

After a scoff, Caleb said, "He's out again?"

Beanie said, "He's been out since Monday. I've called, texted, and emailed several times, but he hasn't responded. He didn't show up for work on Tuesday. Or Wednesday. And now he's not here today. That's not like him."

"Maybe he's sick," suggested Sophie.

"Or, had some emergency and had to leave town," said Stevie.

"Or, maybe he's a lazy, good for nothing who doesn't want to work," complained Caleb as he walked back to his cubicle. "I say good riddance to bad rubbish!"

Shaking his head, Beanie said, "I can't believe he would abandon his internship without any explanation. I need to get in touch with him, someway, and find out what's going on."

After Sophie and Stevie drifted back to their cubicles, Beanie turned to his computer and accessed the *Palmchat Gazette* employee database. Joshua wasn't answering his cell phone, so Beanie looked up the intern's residential landline. He picked up his desk phone and dialed the number.

Six rings later, a male voice, drowsy and thick, said, "Yeah?"

Beanie identified himself, and then said, "I'm trying to reach Joshua Howard."

"Josh ain't here right now," said the tired guy. "Try his cell."

"I have tried his cell phone," said Beanie. "He's not answering my calls or texts."

"He ain't been around for a few days," the guy said. "I don't know where he is."

"When was the last time you saw him?"

"Dude, I don't even remember," said the guy. "Josh takes off without telling anybody sometimes. Goes off the grid a lot. Doesn't keep in touch. Likes to be alone and clear his head, or whatever, you know?"

"So you think he's off the grid somewhere?" asked Beanie.

"Maybe. Probably. Try calling his girlfriend," said the guy. "She keeps him on a short leash. She'll know where he is."

"What's her name?" asked Beanie, reaching for a yellow sticky pad. "Do you have her number?"

The guy coughed, then cleared his throat. "Hold on …"

Minutes later, after reaching Joshua's girlfriend, Beanie introduced himself and said, "I'm trying to get in touch with Joshua. He hasn't been to work in a few days. Do you know where he is or how I can reach him?"

"Oh, my God! I'm so glad you called," she exclaimed, her voice laced with panicked anguish. "We need to talk. I'm so worried. I don't know what to do."

"Wait a minute. Calm down," cautioned Beanie. "What's going on? What are you worried about?"

"I'm worried about Joshua," she said. "I think something bad happened to him!"

5

"Someone probably killed Joshua and cut him into tiny, little pieces."

Beanie stared at Friday H. Smith, the girlfriend of Joshua Howard. Tall and lithe, the brown-skinned island girl wore aqua-colored glasses, an orange skirt, and a yellow blouse. Even more vivid than her outfit, which made Beanie think of highlighter markers, was her hair. Dyed platinum blonde, it was shaved on the sides and long on the top, swerved into a swooping, stiff pompadour. Beanie figured it must have taken an entire bottle of styling gel to hold it in place. Even the errant gusts wafting across the square were no match for the lacquered strands.

After agreeing to meet Joshua's girlfriend at her job—the St. Killian Public Library, Beanie grabbed his keys and phone and headed off. Fifteen minutes after leaving the *Palmchat Gazette*, he found Friday, who worked in the administration department as a financial service clerk, outside in the library's large courtyard. Peaceful and picturesque, the green space was surrounded by palm trees and flowering bougainvillea in vibrant hues of pink and purple. Following introductions, Beanie joined her on a stone bench under a guava tree.

"Why do you think somebody killed him?" asked Beanie, careful to remove any skepticism from his tone, though he doubted Joshua had been murdered. Beanie thought the girlfriend might have a rampant imagination.

When he'd approached the bench where she was taking a break, he'd noticed she was reading a popular psychological thriller. The plot of the novel—which, if Beanie recalled correctly—was about a missing husband. The girlfriend might have thought life was imitating art.

"What else am I supposed to think?" she asked, throwing up her hands with a dramatic flair. "I haven't heard from him in three days."

"When I called his house," said Beanie. "I spoke to someone who said he's known for taking off and not keeping in touch."

"That was probably Joshua's roommate Travis. And he's right. But this time is different," said Friday, leaning toward him, eyes narrowed, voice lowered. "Normally, when Joshua goes off the grid, I usually still hear from him, but this time, there's been no texts or phone calls. I have no idea where he is. He won't return my calls."

Beanie frowned. "That doesn't mean he's dead."

After a frustrated exhale, Friday said, "Okay, fine, maybe he's not dead. But he is missing. Not that the cops believe that."

Shocked, Beanie asked, "You called the police?"

Throwing up her hands again, Friday said, "What else was I supposed to do? I haven't seen my boyfriend in three days! I filed a missing person report. Not that it did any good. They didn't even believe me. They said people are allowed to leave and not tell you where they're going, or whatever."

"That's true," said Beanie, nodding. "The police won't automatically investigate a disappearance unless there's some evidence of foul play, or the person is a minor."

"I told him that when Joshua disappears, he doesn't really disappear," she said. "He just goes to the jungle to smoke weed and clear his head."

Interesting, thought Beanie. Something he hadn't known, or suspected, about Joshua.

"But there's always some sort of communication from him," said Friday. "So why isn't he texting? Why isn't he calling?"

Rubbing his chin, Beanie wasn't sure what to think. Except maybe Friday was right to be worried. Perhaps the intern was missing. But where was the actual proof of that?

"And it's really weird because Joshua only disappears when he's depressed," said Friday, tilting her head back as though contemplating something in the branches of the mango tree above them. "And he wasn't depressed. He was super stoked about getting the internship at the *Palmchat Gazette*."

"Are you sure about that?" asked Beanie. "Because he hasn't shown up at the paper since Monday."

"You know, I should probably start at the beginning," said Friday, tapping a finger against her chin. "So, you can have a clear picture of the events in question and why they don't make sense."

"Okay …" said Beanie, wary of the intensity of Friday's stare.

"As a reporter, you want all the facts, right?" asked Friday, a slight furrow between her arched brows. "So, you can investigate the story and find out what really happened to Joshua."

Clearing his throat, Beanie shifted on the stone bench, which was starting to make his butt numb. "Actually, as a reporter, my job is to report the facts, so I can write a story about them, not to investigate a possible crime. That's what the police do."

Beanie's description of his job duties wasn't entirely accurate. Technically, he did investigate crimes, and when he could, he was willing to help the police bring a criminal to justice if his sleuthing turned up any crucial evidence—which it had in the past. But he didn't want to get Friday's hopes up. She seemed a bit too eager for him to solve the case. Not that Beanie thought there was a case to be solved.

Lips pursed, Friday said, "But reporters can solve crimes. Especially crimes the cops don't care about or take seriously. Like in the book I'm reading, *The Lost Husband*."

Beanie glanced at the cover as Friday held up the hardback copy.

"Have you read it?" asked Friday, her eyes alight with excitement.

Shaking his head, Beanie said, "I usually read non-fiction. True Crime."

"It's really good. You should read it," advised Friday, giving him a wide smile. "Anyway, in the book, the wife asks her ex-boyfriend, a journalist, to look into the case of her missing husband because the cops aren't taking her seriously, which is the same thing that's happening to me."

"Maybe they need more evidence that Joshua has really disappeared," suggested Beanie, wondering if the cops' skepticism had anything to do with Friday's outrageous hair or her melodramatic mannerisms. As much as Beanie wanted to find Joshua, he was already regretting his decision to question Friday about the intern's whereabouts. He had a feeling she'd convinced herself that her life had become a suspense thriller novel. Beanie needed facts, not wild speculation.

"You mind if I consult the notes on my phone?" asked Friday, swiping across the screen of her cell.

"Not at all," said Beanie.

"These are the same notes I gave the cops," said Friday. "I'll email you a copy, as well. Okay, so, I believe it all started on October 29th. That was Monday. I came to pick up Joshua from work when his shift was over."

"You picked him up from the *Palmchat Gazette?*"

"No, from his other job," said Friday.

"Island Parcel, right?" asked Beanie, recalling the intern's part-time paying job. Joshua left the *Palmchat Gazette* each day around three p.m. and headed to the delivery company where he worked a four-hour shift.

"Right," confirmed Friday. "So I picked him up from work at eight p.m. Then we stopped at a food truck for a quick bite. After that, it was around nine o'clock by that time, Joshua asked me to drive him to a friends' house in Oyster Farms, which was strange."

"How so?" asked Beanie, piqued by the mention of his neighborhood.

"I didn't think he knew anybody in Oyster Farms," said Friday. "And when I asked him about the friend, he was really vague and said I didn't know the person. Some friend from school he was working on a project with, he said. So, I tried not to get jealous or let my suspicions run wild because I'm a pretty rational person."

Beanie wasn't sure about that, but if she said so, who was he to dispute it?

Friday went on, "Anyway, Josh told me to drop him off at the neighborhood park, and he would walk to the friend's house because he knows I'm directionally challenged, and he was afraid I wouldn't be able to find my way out of the neighborhood. So, he was supposed to text me to come and pick him up, but he never did. So, I texted him."

"And did he text you back?"

Friday nodded. "But not immediately. It was like an hour later. The text said that he hadn't been feeling well, so the friend drove him home. So, I drove to his house to check on him, but no one was home."

"Interesting," said Beanie, and found that he actually meant it.

"I texted him again to tell him I was at his place, and he wasn't there," she said. "I was worried that maybe he'd had to go to the emergency room or something. But he didn't return the text. I texted a few of his friends that I know, but none of them had heard from him, so I went home and continued to text him. He never texted me, and so I just went to bed."

Beanie took a breath as a balmy breeze wafted through the courtyard, rustling palm fronds. "I know you said you didn't want to get jealous and suspicious but is it possible—"

"That he was cheating on me with another girl that night?" she asked. "Anything is possible, I suppose, but I don't think so. And I'm not trying to ignore any signs. I don't think he went to see another girl. I think he went to see ..."

Wondering why she'd trailed off and looked away, Beanie asked, "Went to see ... who? What were you going to say?"

Shaking her head, Friday said, "I was going to say the cops are not going to bother looking for Joshua because they don't think he's missing, but you can investigate. Just like the reporter in *The Lost Husband*. He's in the process of uncovering a cover-up in the husband's disappearance."

"I can definitely write a story and raise some questions," said Beanie. "But I don't know if—"

"You must think something bad happened to him," she said, her tone not quite beseeching, but almost. "Isn't that why you came to talk to me?"

"I came to ask you if you knew where Joshua was," admitted Beanie, "because I wanted to ask him if he wanted to continue working at the *Palmchat Gazette*. I'm not sure that anything bad happened to Joshua."

"Don't you want to find out?" asked Friday, her gaze imploring. "He's your intern. Don't you want to know what happened to him?"

"Joshua is not *my* intern," Beanie felt the need to clarify. "He worked for all of the reporters at the paper."

"But you're the only one he liked," said Friday. "He told me that you were really cool. And he was learning so much from you. Now he's missing, and you don't care?"

Feeling like a calloused heel, Beanie said, "Of course, I care. I don't think anything bad happened to Joshua, but you're right. I need to find out where he is and what's going on with him … "

6

Later that afternoon, at his desk with his third cup of coffee, Beanie turned to his computer and opened a Word file.

Despite his belief that nothing terrible had happened to Joshua, Beanie wanted to find the intern. For one, he wanted to find out if Joshua was still interested in keeping his internship at the *Palmchat Gazette*. And for two, he hoped to prove that Joshua's girlfriend was jumping to dire conclusions for nothing. And, admittedly, if only to himself, Beanie wanted to prevent any doubts or suspicions he might develop about the intern's well-being.

Resolved to his task, he decided to retrace the student's steps.

According to his notes, the last time anyone had seen or heard from Joshua was on October 29th, when he'd completed his shift at Island Parcel. Friday claimed to have picked him up from work and then driven him to Oyster Farms to meet a friend.

A friend Friday didn't know. Maybe another woman. Maybe someone a co-worker friend might know about. Beanie opened a new Internet browser and searched for the number to Island Parcel Pick-Up. Ten minutes later, he was on the phone with Dan Chevalier, the owner.

"I can't talk very long," began Chevalier, his tone laced with caution.

Beanie pegged him as someone who didn't want to get involved, but still wanted to reveal what he knew, and maybe offer an opinion.

"I won't take up too much of your time," promised Beanie. "Just wanted to ask you a few questions about one of your employees."

"I don't got all day to talk," warned Chevalier. "But I'll try to answer your question as best I can."

Beanie said, "I'm trying to locate Joshua Howard—"

"You and me both," said Chevalier. "He missed his shift yesterday, and he's on the schedule today, but I don't know if he's going to show up. I've been calling, but he's not answering or calling me back."

Concerned, Beanie said, "He's missed a few days here at the paper where he's interning."

"I'll tell you what," said Chevalier. "He misses work tonight, and he's fired."

Beanie cleared his throat. "Mr. Chevalier, I've been able to determine that the last time anyone saw Joshua was on October 29th. Was that the last day he showed up for work?"

"I think so," said Chevalier. "I'd have to check with my secretary to make sure, but I remember it was a couple days before Halloween."

Turning to his computer, Beanie typed notes into his Word file. "Did you talk to him on October 29th?"

"I'm sure I did," said Chevalier. "I was always having to talk to Howard. Having to reprimand him. Remind him to do his job. He wasn't exactly the best employee."

"How do you mean?" asked Beanie, though he wasn't surprised to learn something else about Joshua that he hadn't known, or suspected.

"Had to write him up for going off route a few times," said Chevalier.

"Going off route?" asked Beanie, unfamiliar with the phrase.

"All my drivers got a route assigned to them," said the owner. "They need to stay on that route and don't veer off it, you understand? Don't deviate from it."

"Joshua veered from his route?"

"A couple of times," said Chevalier. "Joshua's route was Little Turkey. But, several times, while on duty, he was over in Oyster Farms."

"What was he doing in Oyster Farms?" asked Beanie, recalling that Joshua's girlfriend had driven him to Oyster Farms on October 29th.

"I don't know," grunted Chevalier. "Probably something he didn't have no business doing."

"Mr. Chevalier, how did you know that Joshua was veering off route?" asked Beanie. "How did you know he was in Oyster Farms?"

"Got GPS on some of my trucks," said the owner. "Not all of them, but on the ones that do, I check the GPS to make sure my drivers are where they're supposed to be. Twice last month, Howard's truck was parked in Oyster Farms when he should have been making deliveries in Little Turkey."

"Was there GPS in the truck Howard was driving on October 29th?"

"I think so, but I can't be sure," said Chevalier. "My drivers don't use the same trucks every day, and like I said, I don't got GPS in all of them. I'd have to check. Hold on ..."

In the silence, Beanie heard fingers tapping on a keyboard.

Chevalier said, "Okay, so, looks like the truck Joshua was driving on October 29th did have GPS. And he went off route again."

"You have the address where he went?"

Chevalier said, "Last address he went to that day was ... 3110 Dolphin Lane."

At the mention of the street where he and his family lived, Beanie experienced a jolt of surprise. "3110 Dolphin Lane. Are you sure?"

"I'm looking right at the computer logs," said Chevalier. "That's what it says. Arrived at that address around seven o'clock. Stayed about twenty minutes. What he was doing there, I have no idea. But he wasn't delivering or picking up a package. Probably fooling around with some girl on company time."

"Thanks for checking," said Beanie, distracted as he made a note of the address.

Chevalier said, "What's funny about Howard being in Oyster Farms is that he told me he didn't want to go back to that neighborhood."

"Why not?"

"Last thing I wrote him up for was for refusing to deliver a package in Oyster Farms," said Chevalier. "Claimed he was attacked. He wasn't even supposed to be in Oyster Farms in the first place, but he was switching routes with another driver."

Curious, Beanie asked, "Who attacked him?"

"He didn't say," said the owner. "I figured some dog got after him."

"And the attack happened in Oyster Farms?"

"House on Dolphin Lane. Might have been the same one where he was at on October 29th," said the owner. "Listen, can you call back? We're busy and—"

"Sure, no problem," said Beanie, distracted by the details Chevalier had given him. "Thanks for talking to me. I appreciate it."

After ending the call with the delivery company owner, Beanie stared at the address he'd written.

3110 Dolphin Lane. The last house Joshua had visited when he'd veered off his schedule on October 29th, the last day anyone had seen or heard from him. Why had Joshua gone off route to that house? He hadn't been scheduled to deliver a package to that specific residence. So why had he gone there? Did he know who lived there? Did Joshua's mysterious friend live at 3110 Dolphin Lane?

Beanie leaned back in his chair and exhaled.

There was only way to find out.

He had to talk to the people who lived at 3110 Dolphin Lane.

Ivan and Natalya Volkov.

7

An hour later, Beanie turned left onto Dolphin Lane.

Driving past his own house, a pale-yellow bungalow with white trim, he stayed five miles under the posted speed limit of twenty miles per hour as he approached the Volkovs' house. Parking the SUV along the curb, Beanie cut the ignition. Outside of his SUV, a salty, balmy breeze wafted across his face, cooling the sweat on his brow.

After a quick exhale, Beanie was about to head up the pathway to the Volkov's house when he heard someone shouting his name behind him.

Curious, Beanie turned.

And groaned to himself.

Mr. Mendez strolled toward him. Dressed in a pink short-sleeved cotton shirt and turquoise Bermuda shorts, he held what looked like a rolled-up newspaper, which he waved back and forth in greeting. "How are you doing?"

Beanie exhaled. He didn't have time to shoot the breeze with Mendez, a man who was known to share unwanted information about his robust love life.

"I'm working on a story," said Beanie.

"About the Volkovs?" asked Mendez, glancing towards the coral bungalow.

Reluctant to confide in Mendez, who wasn't as gossipy as Old Wilson but wasn't above starting unfounded rumors, Beanie said, "I just wanted to ask them a few questions."

Nodding, Mendez said, "I heard their dog attacked your boys on Halloween."

"Yeah, it was a few scary moments," said Beanie, rubbing a hand down the back of his head as memories of the snarling Husky flooded his mind.

"But you know it wasn't really the dog, right?"

Beanie glanced at Mendez. "What do you mean?"

"It was the wife," said Mendez, squinting in the harsh, bright, late-afternoon St. Killian sun.

"The wife?" asked Beanie, confused.

Mendez asked, "Have you seen her eyes?"

Beanie felt the odd chill again. "Yeah, so …"

"So have you noticed that their dog has the same eyes?" asked Mendez.

Beanie had noticed, but he'd tried not to dwell on it. "Okay, and … what?"

"Don't you wonder why the wife and the dog have the same eyes?"

"Hadn't really thought about it," remarked Beanie, leaning against the SUV door.

"Don't you wonder why you never see the wife and the dog together?"

Beanie shook his head. "Not really."

"It's because the wife and the dog are one and the same," declared Mendez.

Holding in his annoyed exhale, Beanie asked, "What are you talking about?"

"The wife is the dog," insisted Mendez. "The wife is a shapeshifter."

Beanie frowned. "Shapeshifter?"

"You know what that is?" asked Mendez. "People who can—"

"Yeah, I know what a shapeshifter is," said Beanie, finding it hard to believe that he was actually having the conversation. "What I don't know is, why do you think the wife … no, you know what? Never mind."

"You know why the dog attacked your boys?" asked Mendez. "Because the wife is the dog and she needs to feed. Probably on human flesh."

Rubbing his eyes, Beanie sighed. "Mr. Mendez, I don't think the wife is a dog."

"But you don't know that she isn't," countered Mendez. "I believe she is, and I think she's been roaming the neighborhood biting people."

"You actually think that?" asked Beanie, folding his arms.

"That's what Old Wilson told me," said Mendez.

"Old Wilson thinks Mrs. Volkov shifts into a Siberian husky and bites people?" asked Beanie, shocked that he'd even asked the question.

"Old Wilson told me about the wolf biting people in the neighborhood," said Mendez. "But I know it's not a wolf. It's Mrs. Volkov. And I have proof."

Skeptical, Beanie stared at the man. "You have proof that Mrs. Volkov is a wolf?"

"I'm sure I do," said Mendez. "I'm sure I have video surveillance of her changing from a woman into a wolf. I'm still reviewing the footage from my security system."

"Your security system?" asked Beanie, mildly surprised. "You have cameras around your house?"

"An extensive network of exterior cameras," said Mendez, beaming with pride. "It's state of the art. Top of the line. The cameras record all day every day in fifteen-minute loops. I've set it up so that each fifteen-minute loop is downloaded and saved to the external hard drive on my computer as a video file."

"Wow," said Beanie. Most residents in Oyster Farms didn't have video cameras to monitor suspicious activity and relied on the vigilance of the neighborhood watch group.

"On the weekends," said Mendez, "I review the video files. If I see anything untoward, I forward the video to the police. Right now, however, as I said, I need to find video of Mrs. Volkov to prove she's a shapeshifter."

Beanie contemplated asking Mendez what he would do if he found the footage but decided he didn't want to encourage the man's tomfoolery. "Okay, well, good luck with that."

Mendez said, "I'll let you know what I find."

As Mendez walked away, Beanie turned and walked up the path to Ivan Volkov's house. What Mendez had told him was ridiculous. Beanie did not believe for one minute that the wife could morph into a Siberian husky. He couldn't believe he'd entertained Mendez's rampant foolishness.

At the door, he raised his hand to knock against the wood. Moments later, the door opened. Volkov's wife, Natalya, stared up at him with those cold, ice-blue eyes.

"Mrs. Volkov, I don't mean to bother you," began Beanie, taking a step back as the woman stepped out onto the porch.

Pale and trembling, Natalya Volkov held her thin hand at her neck, as though protecting her throat. Shaking her head, she said, "It is fine. Tell me, please, how are little boys? They are not still scared because of dog?"

"The boys are fine, thank you for asking," said Beanie. "Listen, I just wanted to ask you about an investigation I'm working on."

"Yes, you work for paper." She gave him a slight smile and nodded. "I have read stories you write. You are good journalist."

"Thanks, I appreciate that," said Beanie. "One of the stories I'm working on is about a university student who may have disappeared. He worked for a company called Island Parcel Pick-Up. I spoke to the owner of the company who said that the student delivered a package to your home a few weeks ago, and—"

"No, no, is not true!" exclaimed Natalya Volkov, shaking her head violently.

Shocked by her vehement response, Beanie said, "Mrs. Volkov, I just wanted to ask you if—"

"Was wrong house," said Volkov's wife, clutching her throat, the veins in her bony hand rising like thin coils of rope beneath her translucent, papery skin.

"Can you tell me if this was the delivery driver?" asked Beanie, holding his phone in front of her. While she'd been denying receiving a package, he'd found a photo of Joshua he'd downloaded from the *Palmchat Gazette*'s website, which featured the students who interned at the paper each semester.

Natalya Volkov's eyes widened as she stared at the phone.

Beanie caught a flash of recollection in her strange, glowing irises, but Volkov's wife gave her head another violent shake. "I do not remember."

"Are you sure?" asked Beanie, skeptical of her claim. "His name is Joshua Howard. Maybe if I enlarge the photo, you can—"

"Joshua Howard." Natalya shook as she looked away.

"You recognize that name?" asked Beanie, suspecting she did.

"No, I … do not know," she said, her voice whispery and halting. "I do not know him. I am sure. And now I must go. I am sorry I cannot help you find him. I do not know where he went after …"

"After … what?" prompted Beanie, convinced the woman knew more about Joshua than she was telling him.

"I am sorry he is gone, but I do not know where he is," she said, as dark pink splotches appeared on her cheeks and chin. "I do not … I need … water … must have water."

"Mrs. Volkov, are you okay?"

The wife turned and rushed into the house, leaving the door open. Cursing, Beanie slipped his phone back into the front pocket of his pants. Natalya Volkov had lied to him, Beanie was sure of it. Joshua's photo and his name had evoked a visceral reaction in the woman. She knew exactly who Joshua was. And Beanie figured she knew more than that. What she knew had made her nervous. So nervous she'd broken out in hives. Beanie didn't want to leave without asking her more questions, but—

A strange growling gave Beanie a start. What the—

A glass crashed.

"Mrs. Volkov?" Beanie called out. "Everything okay?"

More snarling. Was it the dog? Against his better judgment, Beanie pushed the door open wider and peered into the darkened living room.

The huge Siberian husky lunged toward him, growling and snarling. Not again, thought Beanie, panic racing through him as he prepared to turn and flee.

"No! Stop!" the harsh commands came from behind him. "Sit!"

Beanie turned. Ivan Volkov strode toward the dog. Grabbing the husky by her collar, he spoke harshly to the animal as he took it out of the room. Minutes later, Ivan and Natalya reappeared, giving Beanie contrite looks as they apologized profusely and promised to make sure the husky never threatened him again.

Moments later, as Beanie hurried toward his car, he couldn't help thinking of what Mendez had said.

You never see the wife and the dog together.

Hours later, following dinner and then bath and bedtime stories with their boys, Beanie cuddled with his wife in their king-sized bed to continue discussing his strange afternoon.

"I can't believe Natalya Volkov broke out into hives," said Noelle, snuggling close to Beanie.

"Neither could I," said Beanie. "If I hadn't seen it myself, I probably wouldn't believe it."

Noelle said, "Why were you talking to Natalya anyway? Did you tell me?"

"We discussed it over dinner," said Beanie, opening his eyes to gaze at his gorgeous wife.

"Hmmm …" Noelle sighed. "Maybe I wasn't paying attention. The boys were extra rowdy tonight. I have to tell Mom to stop buying them snow cones from the ice cream truck. Anyway, tell me again about why you talked to her."

"I wanted to ask her why Joshua went to her house on October 29th," said Beanie.

"What did she say?"

Beanie sighed. "Didn't get a chance to ask her. I mentioned that Joshua had delivered a package to their house a few weeks ago, and she immediately started with the denials."

Rolling over and propping her head against the pillows stacked behind them, Noelle asked, "So, you think the Volkovs are Joshua's mysterious friends who live in Oyster Farms?"

"I'm not sure. Joshua went to see them before his shift ended, but it wasn't to deliver a package," said Beanie. "Then when he got off work, he told his girlfriend, Friday—"

"His girlfriend … Friday?" echoed Noelle. "Joshua's girlfriend's name is Friday? As in, thank God it's …"

"Friday," confirmed Beanie, recalling the eccentric young woman. "And, trust me, it sort of fits her personality. Anyway, Joshua told Friday to drive him back to Oyster Farms and drop him off at the park."

"And you think he walked to the Volkov's house?"

"Yeah, and if that's true, then the question is why?" asked Beanie. "Why did he go to the Volkovs before his shift ended? Why did he return after his shift? That's what I don't know. What I do know is that Natalya recognized Joshua. I showed her his photo on my phone, and I could tell she'd seen him before."

"Maybe you should ask Joshua's girlfriend if he knows the Volkovs," suggested Noelle.

"Maybe I should, but ..."

"But what?"

Beanie chuckled softly. "She's a little ... out there ..."

"Out there?" asked Noelle. "What does that mean?"

"A little too melodramatic," said Beanie. "She's convinced something bad happened to Joshua. She filed a missing person report. She wants me to investigate his disappearance."

"What if she's right?" asked Noelle. "What if something bad did happen to Joshua?"

"Elle ..." cautioned Beanie.

"You think his girlfriend is overreacting?"

"I think Friday is being influenced by this book she's reading. It's about a woman whose husband goes missing, and a reporter helps her find him or something."

"What's the name of it?" asked Noelle.

"*The Lost Husband*, I think," said Beanie.

"I read that book," said Noelle. "My co-worker told me about it."

"Did you like it?" asked Beanie.

"It was pretty good." Noelle shrugged. "Turns out, the wife killed the husband."

Staring at his wife, Beanie asked, "Wait, what? Are we talking about the same book?"

"I'm pretty sure we are," said Noelle.

"Joshua's girlfriend said the wife reported her husband missing and then got some reporter friend to help her when the cops wouldn't take her seriously."

Noelle said, "She was lying. The wife was one of those unreliable narrators. She ended up killing the journalist, too."

Beanie rubbed his jaw. "Well, that puts things in a different light."

"How so?"

"What if Joshua's girlfriend is an unreliable narrator?" asked Beanie. "How do I know she's telling me the truth?"

"For all you know," said Noelle. "She might have Joshua locked up somewhere. She might even start sending texts from Joshua to herself to make it look like he's missing."

Beanie frowned. "That's weird. Why would she do that?"

Noelle said, "Well, that's what happened in the book. The wife went beyond a double-cross. It was more like a quadruple cross."

"A quadruple cross?"

Noelle said, "You have to read it to understand, but basically, nothing the wife said was real. Everything she told the police and the reporter was designed to fool them into thinking she was telling the truth."

"Interesting," said Beanie, not sure what to think as he reflected on Joshua's girlfriend and her seeming fascination with *The Lost Husband*. He wondered if it might be best to leave any investigating to the police.

8

Backing out of his driveway the next morning, Beanie thought about Joshua's girlfriend and contemplated calling her to ask if Joshua knew Ivan and Natalya Volkov. He wasn't in the mood for more of Friday's histrionic behavior, but if Joshua had some association with the Russian couple, and Friday could provide answers, then—

Up ahead, three houses down, on the right, something caught Beanie's eye, intruding on his thoughts. His attention arrested by the scene, Beanie slowed the SUV to a crawl, trying to figure out what was going on in the front yard of the Volkov's house.

There seemed to be some commotion between Volkov, his wife, and ... was that Old Wilson? Whatever was happening was contentious. Old Wilson looked as though he was fussing about something while the Volkovs shook their heads.

Beanie pulled up next to the curb in front of the Volkov's home and exited the SUV, closing the door behind him.

"That beast bit me!" bellowed Old Wilson, his wrinkled face contorted in anger. "I'm calling the cops!"

"Please, no, there is no need to involve police," said Volkov, his expression pained. "We can make this right between us as neighbors."

"We will pay for your visit to doctor," said Natalya, one hand clutching her throat, the other grasping her husband's forearm. "We are so sorry this happened!"

"What's going on?" asked Beanie, approaching his neighbors.

Old Wilson held up his left hand, which was wrapped in a swath of white cloth soaked through with blood.

"Our dog bit him," said Volkov, his gaze imploring as he stared at Beanie. "It was accident."

"That ain't what happened," said Old Wilson, glaring at the Volkovs. "And it wasn't an accident!"

"The dog, she is frightened by people she does not know," said Natalya. "And she bites."

"They're lying," said Old Wilson, grimacing as he turned and walked away. "I'm calling the police! I'm having you arrested!"

"No, you cannot," said Ivan. "Please don't!"

"Can you talk to him?" Natalya asked Beanie. "He is your friend. Please explain we never mean for this to happen!"

Exhaling, Beanie stared at the couple. "Where is the dog now?"

"She is inside house," said Volkov. "She is in spare bedroom. We have locked door, so she cannot get out and hurt anyone."

"As I told you, this is a neighborhood with lots of small children and old people," said Beanie. "This is no place for an aggressive dog, so maybe you should get rid of it—"

"Never!" declared Ivan, his jaw clenched tight, eyes shining with manic rage as his body trembled.

Shocked by the man's vehemence, Beanie took a step back.

Natalya's glowing ice-blue eyes shifted from her husband to Beanie. She said, "The dog is very important to us. She is family. We have had her since she is born. We cannot abandon her, but we can make sure she is not a threat to anyone. Please tell Mr. Wilson that."

Not willing to make the Volkovs any promises, Beanie turned from the couple and walked back toward his SUV. Old Wilson was heading toward his house. Beanie jogged to catch up with the widower.

"Mr. Wilson," said Beanie, falling in step with his neighbor. "How's your hand?"

Scoffing, Old Wilson said, "Nearly bit my hand clean off!"

"Listen, let me take you to the emergency room," said Beanie, placing a hand on the man's shoulder, slowing his progress.

"I don't need no doctor," grumbled Old Wilson. "I can take care of it myself. I was a medic in 'Nam. I put men back together that had their arms and legs blown off. I can stitch up my own hand."

Beanie said, "But still, you need to be checked for rabies."

Stopping at the end of his driveway, Old Wilson stared at Beanie, his expression bewildered. "Why should I be checked for rabies?"

"That crazy Siberian husky bit you," said Beanie, glancing at the old man's injured hand. "I think the Volkov's dog is that wolf people in the neighborhood think they've seen."

"It wasn't the dog that bit me!" said Old Wilson, shaking his head.

"What are you talking about?"

Old Wilson let out an exasperated sigh. "I'm talking about Volkov's wife. She bit me!"

Beanie stared at the caustic old widower. "Did you just say—"

"Volkov's wife bit me!" Old Wilson huffed. "And I ain't the only one she's sunk her teeth into! Ask Mendez. He'll tell you! He says she's really a dog, and she needs to feed, and I believe him."

"Mr. Wilson, I don't really think—"

"She bit Mr. Turner and Mrs. Washington on Shark Avenue," insisted Old Wilson. "They thought it was a wolf that bit them, but that wasn't true. It ain't no wolf biting people! It's her!"

***

"You don't really believe that, do you?" asked Sophie, frowning.

Wide-eyed, Stevie asked, "Your neighbor can shapeshift into a Siberian Husky?"

After a sip of his second cup of coffee that morning, Beanie shook his head. "Of course, I don't. A person can't shapeshift into an animal."

Stevie said, "I beg to differ ..."

Rolling her eyes, Sophie said, "I meant, do you believe your neighbor bit your other neighbor?"

"Can't believe that instead of working, the three of you are talking about folks biting other folks! I don't have time for this ignorant foolishness!" Caleb exclaimed as he turned and walked away from Beanie's cubicle, where Beanie had gathered his three closest coworkers that morning. "Folks ain't got nothing better to do than engage in nonsense!"

Beanie focused on Sophie and Stevie. "I agree with Caleb. It's foolishness."

"Ignorant foolishness," clarified Sophie, pursing her lips.

"That's the same look my wife gave me last night," confessed Beanie. "She didn't believe me and didn't want to entertain all this ridiculousness, which I tried to explain to her."

"Explain it to us," requested Stevie, his expression suggesting a willingness to be open-minded.

"There's nothing to explain," said Sophie, taking a sip of coffee from the paper cup she held. "A person can't shapeshift into an animal. But, a person can bite another person."

"I don't know if Natalya bit Old Wilson's hand," said Stevie. "That's what he claims, but I think it was the dog."

"Why would your neighbor Old Wilson lie about the wife biting him?" asked Sophie.

"Maybe the dog attacked Old Wilson," said Beanie. "But when Natalya was trying to get the dog away from him, the dog bit Old Wilson, but he couldn't tell if it was Natalya or the dog who'd bitten him."

"That's possible, I suppose," said Sophie. "But why would Old Wilson assume the wife had bitten him? You'd think he'd assume the dog had bitten him."

Beanie scoffed. "You don't know Old Wilson."

Stevie asked, "Why do you think your neighbor is a shapeshifter?"

"I don't think that," said Beanie, though he wasn't sure what he thought. "My other neighbors, Mr. Mendez and Old Wilson think our new neighbors, Ivan and Natalya Volkov, can shapeshift. Well, the wife can turn into a dog."

"And why does he think this?" asked Sophie, scowling.

"Ivan and Natalya have a Siberian Husky," said Beanie. "The dog has ice-blue eyes that almost glow. Natalya's eyes are ice-blue, and they also seem to glow. So, Mendez thinks the wife and the dog are the same."

Stevie nodded. "I can see that."

Sophie shook her head. "Maybe the wife is wearing colored contact lenses. Some people are obsessive about their dogs and even want to look like their animals."

Nodding, Beanie considered Sophie's rational explanation. "But, then, Mr. Mendez pointed out to me that the wife and the dog are never seen at the same time. If you see the wife, the dog isn't around and vice versa. When I was trick or treating with the boys, the Husky lunged at us. Ivan Volkov stopped the attack and sent the dog into the house. A minute later, Natalya came out of the house."

Stevie said, "She went into the house as the dog and came out in her human female form."

"Don't be ridiculous," Sophie said, rolling her eyes. "Anyway. So still no word on where Joshua might be?"

Beanie shook his head. "Not yet. His family and friends haven't heard anything. Nobody knows where he is or if anything happened to him."

After talking to Friday, who believed Joshua's disappearance was the result of foul play and had filed a missing person report, Beanie had written a story detailing what little he knew. Even with few scant details, the story, *UNIVERSITY STUDENT FEARED MISSING*, had garnered lots of clicks and had great read through. Engagement from readers was positive, with several hundred comments and a fair number of shares on social media sites.

"No leads from the story you wrote?" asked Stevie.

"Fields told me that people are calling the police station claiming to have seen Joshua here or there," said Beanie. "Nothing has panned out yet."

"And you still don't know who he went to visit in Oyster Farms that night?" asked Sophie.

Shaking his head, Beanie said, "No one in the neighborhood knows. My wife told me there's been some discussion on a few of the Oyster Farms social media sites. Nobody remembers seeing him around, but ..."

"But?" prompted Stevie.

Beanie said, "But I think one of my neighbors is lying about not recognizing Joshua."

"Which one?" asked Sophie.

"Natalya Volkov," said Beanie.

"The shapeshifter?" asked Stevie, a glint of excitement in his gaze.

"I'm gonna slap you," Sophie warned Stevie, then asked Beanie, "Why do you think she's lying? You think she knows Joshua?"

Beanie told Sophie and Stevie about Joshua's visit to the Volkovs on October 29th before his shift ended, then relayed the details of his failed attempt to question Natalya.

"She totally recognized Joshua," said Sophie. "And the fact that she lied about it makes me think she had something to do with his disappearance."

"Wait a minute," cautioned Beanie, holding up a hand. "We can't jump to that conclusion."

Sophie frowned. "Why not? I mean, why would Natalya lie if she doesn't have something to hide?"

Stevie said, "Maybe she doesn't want anyone to know that she shapeshifted into a wolf and ate Joshua."

Groaning, Sophie asked, "Did you seriously just say that?"

Shaking his head, Beanie said, "I think I'm going to slap you now."

***

Following lunch from his favorite food truck in Pourciau Square—the Nanny Goat—Beanie worked on fact-checking a few articles, but his mind wondered.

He couldn't stop thinking about Old Wilson's assertion that Natalya Volkov had bit him or Mendez's claim that Natalya was a shapeshifter. Neither man's account could possibly be factual. Could it? There was no way he could be convinced that the men were telling the truth. Not that he thought the widowers were lying. Mendez and Wilson were convinced of their beliefs. Beliefs Beanie couldn't conceive of as being even remotely possible. And yet, odd doubts swirled in his head. Doubts that bothered him. Doubts about Natalya, her ice-blue eyes, and the strange, sudden attack of hives she'd suffered.

The woman was not a shapeshifter who turned into a Siberian husky to feed.

Beanie could prove it. Or, rather, he wanted to prove that Mendez and

Old Wilson were wrong. Wanted to prove the husky—mistaken for a wolf—was the true culprit.

Remembering Wilson's claims that other people in Oyster Farms had been bitten, Beanie turned to his computer and accessed the webpage of the St. Killian police department's blotter, the daily report of arrests and incidents.

He started his search a few weeks before Halloween and looked for situations involving animal attacks or dog bites in Oyster Farms. Half an hour later, with a list of five incidents, he went to the police department's news report page, where incidents were written like newspaper articles, with more details than the blotter.

After reading the incident reports, Beanie was more disturbed than doubtful.

"You okay …?"

Startled, Beanie glanced away from the computer screen. Stevie stood in the space between the four-foot-high walls of Beanie's tiny cubicle.

"Huh?"

Stevie said, "You look a little spooked."

"I am a little spooked," said Beanie.

Stevie lumbered into the cubicle and plopped down in the chair adjacent to Beanie's desk. "What's going on?"

Beanie exhaled. "Remember I told you and Sophie about the wolf sightings in Oyster Farms."

Nodding, Stevie said, "Only it's not a wolf. It's your neighbor who shapeshifts into a Siberian husky."

Resisting the urge to ball up a piece of paper and throw it at Stevie, Beanie said, "I was trying to prove that it was a dog and not my neighbor who shapeshifts into a Siberian husky, which by the way, isn't true."

"How were you going to prove it?"

"Old Wilson said other neighbors had been bitten," said Beanie. "Figured I'd check the police blotter. See if any of them called the police."

"What did you find out?"

"There were five calls about wolf sightings, and they all occurred at night," began Beanie.

Stevie said, "That does sound spooky."

Beanie gave Stevie a look. "That's not the spooky part. The spooky part is that each of the victims reported seeing a pale, thin woman with strange eyes before being attacked by the wolf."

"They saw your neighbor before she shifted," said Stevie.

"It's more likely that they saw Natalya before she lost control of her dog, and it attacked them," said Beanie, determined to remain rational.

Stevie gave him a dubious look.

Beanie ignored it and turned back to his computer. "Listen to this account: Mamie Kitteridge of 3319 Sharkfin Drive said she was out one night after ten o'clock looking for one of her cats. She was calling for the cat as she walked down the sidewalk of her street. She had just passed a vacant house when she heard a strange growling sound that seemed to be coming from the side of the vacant house. Then she heard a horrible mewling sound, which to Mrs. Kitteridge sounded like a cat being strangled. She cautiously approached the side of the vacant house. The growling sounds increased."

"What was the growling sound?" asked Stevie.

"I'm getting to that," said Beanie. "Though it was dark, Mrs. Kitteridge told police that she could faintly make out the shape of a large wolf – her words – which appeared to be feeding on a much smaller animal, which she feared was her cat. She was terrified and unsure of what to do, so she hurried back to the sidewalk and was going to another neighbor's house to ask for help. As she was hurrying away from the vacant house, she looked back and saw a strange woman running from the side of the vacant house. Mrs. Kitteridge called out to the woman, hoping the woman would help her scare away the wolf. Mrs. Kitteridge says the woman looked back at her but then turned and continued to run away. She says the only thing she remembers about the woman was that she had strange eyes. Later, Mrs. Kitteridge and her neighbor, Mr. Baker, found Mrs. Kitteridge's cat on the side of the vacant house. The cat had been ripped to shreds, according to Mrs. Kitteridge. Torn apart, reported Mr. Baker."

"The woman with the strange eyes was Natalya Volkov," said Stevie.

"I'm sure it was," said Beanie, reflecting on the details of the Kitteridge incident.

"But what happened to the wolf?" asked Stevie.

Beanie glanced at him. "What?"

"The report said Mrs. Kitteridge saw a woman with strange eyes running from the side of the house," said Stevie. "It doesn't say the woman with the strange eyes was running with a wolf. Or a Siberian husky that was mistaken for a wolf."

"Just because the report doesn't say that doesn't mean … " Beanie trailed off, not sure what to think about Stevie's observation, which he hadn't considered, except that it bothered him.

"You really think Natalya ran off and left her husky behind?"

"I don't think so," said Beanie, remembering how the Volkovs had referred to the husky as part of their family.

"So when the pale woman with the strange eyes ran off, where was the wolf all the neighbors had previously seen?" asked Stevie. "Did the wolf disappear? I don't think so. Your neighbors didn't see the wolf because Natalya had already shifted back into her human form."

9

"I've meant to call you, but I've been busy," said Officer Damon Fields. "You got a minute?"

A policeman with the St. Killian PD, Fields was an unofficial anonymous source for the Palmchat Gazette, and an easy-going, affable guy Beanie considered a friend.

"Yeah. What's going on?" asked Beanie as he pressed the 'speaker' function on his desk phone.

"Got some information about Joshua Howard."

"Did you find him?" asked Beanie, his pulse racing in anticipation.

With no word from Joshua in the past six days, Beanie had, admittedly, grown somewhat concerned. Not necessarily worried, though. He wasn't frantic like Joshua's girlfriend, who thought the intern was dead. Nor was he nonchalant like Joshua's roommate, who believed Joshua was somewhere off the grid, clearing his head. Beanie figured there was a logical explanation for the intern's disappearance. An explanation the Volkovs might be able to provide.

Beanie still believed the Volkovs were the last people to have any contact with Joshua on October 29th.

The GPS in the delivery truck Joshua had driven on October 29th had traced the vehicle to the Volkovs house, and Beanie was certain Natalya had recognized the intern. Further reflection on his conversation with Natalya sparked a memory within Beanie. Natalya had slipped and said she didn't know where Joshua had gone after …

The woman had trailed off, but for Beanie, the unfinished sentence was proof Joshua had been at the little peach-colored bungalow.

And yet, his convictions wavered.

Had the Volkovs been the last to see Joshua on October 29th? Were they the mysterious friends? After being dropped off at the park in Oyster Farms, had Joshua walked to 3110 Dolphin Lane?

Beanie didn't know. There was no definitive proof. In the absence of hard facts, there was only conjecture and speculation. As a journalist, he often used deductive reasoning to develop a theory, but the theory had to be tested. Proven.

Officer Fields said, "Not exactly …"

Confused, Beanie asked, "What does that mean? Not exactly?"

"Remember the finger you found in Ethan's candy pail on Halloween?"

"How could I forget?" asked Beanie, though he'd lost interest in the mystery of the severed finger once the mystery of Joshua's whereabouts had taken precedence in his thoughts.

"Well, we identified it," said Fields. "The finger belongs to Joshua Howard."

Beanie froze, his hand poised over the squared yellow notepad. "What? Joshua Howard? Our intern? The severed finger is his? How do you know? I mean, are you sure?"

"The finger did have a print," said Fields. "We ran it and got a hit. Joshua Howard."

Confusion battled with the shock slamming through Beanie. "Wait a minute. You had Joshua's fingerprints on file?"

"Joshua was arrested two weeks ago for disorderly conduct."

"Disorderly conduct?" echoed Beanie, disbelief coursing through him. Joshua was an easy-going, friendly guy. One of those people who rarely met a stranger. Beanie couldn't imagine him being disorderly enough to get arrested.

"He started a fight at Curious Mama on October 20th," said Fields. "He was arrested and made bail the next day."

"Are you serious?" asked Beanie, almost stunned speechless.

Fields said, "Oh, and another thing. Joshua's finger wasn't severed. It was bitten off."

Beanie frowned. "The finger was bitten off. Like by a dog or wild animal?"

"Like by a person," said Fields.

"What?" Beanie stared at the phone. "Did you say—"

"The bite was human," confirmed Fields. "We found human saliva in the finger."

Curious and disturbed, Beanie said, "Someone bit Joshua's finger off ..."

"Apparently so," said Fields. "Who bit the finger off? We don't know. Still working on that. We ran the DNA from the saliva but haven't gotten any hits yet."

Still trying to wrap his head around the idea of a person biting Joshua's finger off, Beanie shook his head. He wasn't quite sure what to make of what Fields had told him.

"A human bite changes the case," said Fields. "We're looking at the possibility that Joshua may have been the victim of battery, which is why we'd like to find the guy. I have a feeling that the DNA tests on the saliva are not going to turn up anything. The only person who knows who bit Joshua is Joshua."

Beanie asked Fields to keep him up to date, and the officer promised he would.

After ending the call, Beanie dragged a hand down his jaw.

Mr. Mendez's accusation of Volkov's wife slipped into Beanie's mind. *The wife is the dog, and she needs to feed. Probably on human flesh.* Of course, Beanie didn't believe that. And yet, another memory slipped into his mind. Joshua's refusal to deliver a package to a house in Oyster Farms. Was it possible that Joshua had been attacked at a home located on Dolphin Lane? Maybe the Volkov's house? Beanie wondered if the Volkov's dog had lunged at Joshua. Or, maybe ...

Beanie shook his head, disturbed by the thought that floated into his head. Could Joshua have been bitten by Natalya Volkov? But, if so, wouldn't Joshua have reported it to the police?

Beanie wondered if he should have shared Mendez' theory of Natalya

Volkov with Officer Fields, and then realized he couldn't have repeated the man's nonsense. Not only was there no proof, but it didn't make sense. Humans couldn't turn into canines. Admittedly, he wondered about Mendez's assertion that the wife and the dog were never around at the same time. An assertion that seemed to be true, but so what?

Resolved to forget about Mendez's wacky theories, Beanie stood, walked to Vivian's office, and repeated what Fields had told him about Joshua's finger. After the Managing Editor requested a follow-up article, Beanie returned to his cubicle, dropped down into his creaky leather chair, and organized his notes.

After determining the angle and direction of the piece, Beanie typed a lead sentence.

St. Killian police confirmed that a finger found in a candy pail on Halloween has been identified as belonging to Joshua Howard, the St. Killian University student missing since October 29th ...

Thirty minutes later, after completing the first draft, Beanie emailed the story, MISSING STUDENT'S FINGER BITTEN OFF, to Vivian's inbox.

That night, after their regular nightly routine of baths and bedtime stories after dinner, Beanie and Noelle tucked Ethan and Evan beneath the covers and lingered in the doorway as the boys' drifted to sleep. Beanie was hoping they would head to their master suite for some sexy time. Instead, Noelle ordered him to follow her into the laundry room, a small, warm space that smelled faintly of bleach but mostly like dryer sheets.

"You're not going to believe what Officer Fields told me about Joshua Howard," said Beanie, staring at his wife as he leaned against the washing machine.

"What?" Noelle reached into the dryer, pulled out a fluffy yellow bath towel, and tossed it at Beanie.

Catching the towel, Beanie asked, "Remember the severed finger we found in the candy pail?"

Noelle made a face. "Don't remind me. What does what Officer Fields told you about Joshua have to do with the severed finger?"

As he folded the bath towel, Beanie said, "The finger belongs to Joshua."

Noelle's mouth dropped open.

"And it wasn't a severed finger," said Beanie. "It was bitten off. By another person."

"Another person?" Noelle asked, gaping at him. "Are you serious?"

"I wish I wasn't."

Noelle pulled more towels from the dryer and dumped them on the folding table. "Do the cops know who bit his finger off?"

"Not yet," said Beanie. "They have DNA from the saliva on the finger, so they're hoping to find a match."

"Do you think …" Noelle started, then shook her head.

"Do I think … what?" prompted Beanie.

Noelle sighed. "You think he's dead?"

Beanie shook his head. "Unlike Friday, I don't believe someone murdered Joshua and cut him up into tiny pieces, but … my thoughts have gone in some odd directions."

"Odd directions?" asked Noelle, holding up a bedsheet. "Help me fold this."

"After Fields told me a person had bitten Joshua's finger off," said Beanie, taking the bottom corners of the sheet. "I thought that maybe Natalya had done it, but that's crazy."

"Or, maybe it isn't," suggested Noelle.

As Noelle took the folded sheet from him, Beanie stared at his wife, wondering if she was losing it. "Elle, of course, it's crazy. Natalya is not turning into a dog and biting people."

"But what if she is?" asked Noelle. "Not turning into a dog, I don't think that. But maybe she bites."

Beanie shook his head. "Why would she bite people? You know what? Never mind."

"But isn't it possible that Natalya bit Joshua's finger off?" asked Noelle. "Old Wilson told you that she bit him."

"Old Wilson is a strange old coot with a bizarre imagination," said Beanie. "He's not exactly credible."

"Okay, then think about this," said Noelle. "When is the last time you saw Joshua?"

Exhaling, Beanie said, "October 29th."

Stacking several towels she'd folded, Noelle asked, "And when he left the paper, all of his fingers were still attached to his hands, right?"

"Yes, they were," said Beanie.

"And according to your conversation with Joshua's boss at Island Parcel," said Noelle, "Joshua went to see the Volkovs thirty minutes before his shift ended."

"If Natalya had bit his finger off, Joshua would have reported that to his boss," said Beanie. "And then I'm sure he would have called the cops and gone to the hospital."

"But remember that Joshua's girlfriend drove him back to Oyster Farms later that night."

Beanie glanced at his wife. "Remember that his girlfriend doesn't know who Joshua went to visit."

"Roland, you said yourself that you think Joshua walked to the Volkovs house that night," said Noelle. "Isn't it possible that Natalya bit Joshua's finger off when he went back to see the Volkovs?"

"Of course, it's possible," said Beanie. "Anything is possible. But is it probable? I don't think so. What reason would she have to bite his finger off?"

"Well, from what you told me," said Noelle, "Joshua wasn't as nice and easy-going as you'd thought. He had a fight at a bar and got arrested."

"There *are* things I don't know about him," conceded Beanie.

"Which means there are things you need to find out," said Noelle, handing him the towels. "Like if something was going on between Joshua and the Volkovs. Some sort of relationship, or something."

Arms laden with fluffy terry cloth, Beanie followed his wife out of the laundry room.

His thoughts were all over the place, from Mendez's ridiculous claims to Old Wilson's ludicrous assertions. Stevie's belief that Natalya was a shapeshifter bothered him, as did his research form the police blotter about the Oyster Farms wolf attacks, which he hadn't mentioned to Noelle because he didn't want to alarm his wife.

Moments later, loading towels in the bathroom linen closet, Beanie considered Noelle's suggestion that Natalya had bit Joshua. He wanted to think he couldn't possibly believe it because it wasn't rational. Because he couldn't think of a reason why Natalya would bite the intern. Seemed illogical. Unnecessarily violent. And very weird. But, just because he couldn't think of a reason didn't mean there wasn't a reason.

Beanie reflected on the surprising things he'd recently learned about Joshua. Things he hadn't known. Things he couldn't believe. The Joshua he'd immediately liked and had eventually gotten to know wouldn't have been fighting in a bar. Or risking his job by being insubordinate. And he certainly wouldn't antagonize a woman to the point where she'd felt her only recourse was to bite his finger off.

Or, would he?

Beanie didn't know. Was there something going on between Joshua and the Volkovs? Some sort of relationship, or something? Maybe. Maybe not.

But he needed to find out.

10

"Got a story for you," said Vivian, walking into Beanie's cubicle.

"What's it about?" asked Beanie.

"Hikers found a dead body in the jungle on the east side of the island," said Vivian. "Grab Stevie, and the two of you go check it out."

"Me and Stevie?" asked Beanie.

"It's time for him to learn the basics of investigative reporting," said Vivian. "I want you to teach him."

"Huh? What?" Beanie gaped at Vivian. "You want me to train Stevie?"

Her gaze just as challenging as her tone, Vivian asked, "Did I stutter?"

Thirty minutes later, Beanie drove with Stevie to the east side of the island, in the lush, verdant tropical rainforest, where nature-loving tourists came to St. Killian to experience its breathtaking natural beauty.

Though still flabbergasted by Vivian's directive that he train Stevie, Beanie was nevertheless determined to do a good job. His boss wouldn't have issued the demand if she didn't think he was up to the challenge. And training Stevie would be a challenge. The nonchalant trust fund slacker was mildly annoying on a good day. There was always the possibility of irritation and frustration with Stevie, but Beanie had a feeling the guy wanted to be a decent reporter.

Beanie turned onto the access road, a one-lane strip of dirt and gravel cut through the rainforest. Normally lined with tour buses, scooters, rental cars, and bikes, the road was a good place to park since there were no designated lots or clearings near the rainforest. That afternoon, the road was crowded with police cars and EMS vehicles.

"There's a spot," pointed out Stevie, indicating a space behind a police squad car. Beanie maneuvered the SUV next to a shallow ditch. After exiting the vehicle, Beanie and Stevie jogged across the road, dodging grooves filled with muddy water from the bands of rains that morning. Beanie showed his press pass to a deputy assigned to keep out unauthorized personnel, and they were directed toward the path that would take them to the dead body.

Pushing aside palm fronds and broad elephant leaves sprinkled with raindrops, Beanie followed Stevie as they headed into the jungle. The body had been discovered by tourists who'd veered off the main trails that most hikers were advised not to stray from.

As he hiked up a small incline, Beanie slapped the back of his sweaty neck, killing a mosquito. The air, stagnant and moist, was trapped beneath a canopy of trees, but now and again, an errant ocean breeze sneaked through the palm fronds.

Moments later, standing in a small clearing beneath tall palm trees, surrounded by the oppressive smell of dead, rotting leaves and leafy foliage, Beanie took notes using an app on his phone as he and Stevie talked to one of the first responders.

"Group of hikers was trying to find the cave where Venus L' Amour kept her victims," said the officer.

Beanie glanced at Stevie, who shared his look of apprehension. The owner of the *Palmchat Gazette*, Leo Bronson, had spent a few horrifying hours in L 'Amour's cave, a natural cavern where she'd kept men, drugged and restrained against their will, before she castrated and then killed them.

"One of the hikers said he heard the Fury had used that same cave decades ago," said the cop, wiping sweat from his forehead. "Crazy some of the crap these tourists want to gawk at. A place where people were dismembered and eaten is a tourist attraction. Ridiculous."

Stevie asked, "You know how the victim died?"

The officer nodded. "Stabbed to death. But the hikers didn't know that when they first came upon the body. They thought some wild animal had attacked the guy."

A frisson of worry snaked through Beanie. "Why'd they think the victim had been attacked by a wild animal?"

"Body was ripped apart," said the officer. "Torn flesh and what appeared to be bite wounds."

"Bite wounds?" echoed Stevie.

Beanie could sense Stevie looking at him, but he wasn't going to entertain any suggestions that the body in the jungle was in any way connected to the alleged wolf attacks reported by the Oyster Farms residents.

"The hikers realized the victim had been stabbed when they turned the body over to give him CPR. That's when they found the knife."

Stevie asked, "The murder weapon was beneath the body?"

Interesting, thought Beanie, making notes in the app on his phone.

Nodding, the officer said, "Yep. Hopefully, we'll get some good prints from it. You want to see the body? Get some pics for your story?"

Moments later, standing between Stevie and the officer, Beanie's pulse raced as he stared at the mangled body in the damp dirt. "I know that guy ..."

"What?" demanded Stevie.

The officer stared at Beanie. "You know the dead man?"

Shaken, his heart slamming, Beanie nodded and whispered, "He's my neighbor ... "

11

"Ivan Volkov is dead," echoed Noelle, sitting across from him at the kitchen table.

Beanie took a sip of the hot chocolate Evan had been too sleepy to finish.

A few hours earlier, after dinner but before their normal bedtime routine, the boys had wanted warm cocoa with marshmallows and whipped crème.

Both tykes had cleaned their plates, including the vegetables, so Noelle was okay with giving them liquid dessert. Ethan drank his chocolaty concoction quickly, downing it like a shot. But Evan wanted to play with the fluffy marshmallows. After a few sips, during which he'd gleefully gotten melted marshmallow all over his face, he laid his head on Beanie's shoulder as his little eyelids fluttered.

Glancing down at Evan's drowsy gaze, Beanie's heart soared. He loved it when little Evan fell asleep in his arms. He always wanted to suspend the moment and savor it, especially on days when he was slammed with horrifying, shocking news.

During the boys' nightly routine—baths followed by a bedtime story—Beanie dreaded telling his wife about Ivan Volkov. Trying to prolong the inevitable, he'd hoped the boys would want him to read two or three of their favorite books. After *Goodnight Moon*, however, both Ethan and Evan went fast to sleep.

Nodding, Beanie said, "He's dead."

"I don't understand," said Noelle. "How is he dead? Why?"

"I wish I knew," said Beanie, staring at his wife. Noelle's shell-shocked silence mirrored the emotions Beanie had been plagued with from the moment he'd recognized the dead man as his odd neighbor, Ivan Volkov.

The officer had given him a shrewd, dubious look. When Volkov's body was further examined, the dead man's wallet was found. The name on the identification card proved Beanie's claim. Immediately, Beanie had been subjected to a tense, terse quasi-interrogation, one which he might have refused if he hadn't been so flabbergasted by the death of Ivan Volkov. Exactly how did you know the deceased? When did you meet him? How long have you known him? When was the last time you saw him? Does he have any enemies that you know of? Does he have any issues with any of the other neighbors on your street?

Beanie had hesitated, unsure how to answer that question. Mr. Mendez was convinced that Natalya was a shapeshifter, but he didn't think the geriatric playboy had ever confronted the Russians. After Old Wilson had accused Natalya of biting his hand, there had been bad blood between the widower and the odd couple. Beanie couldn't fathom Old Wilson stabbing Volkov and ripping the man's body apart, though. Beanie didn't think the old guy had the stamina or the strength to carry out such a violent, vicious murder. Beanie had shaken his head and told the officers he wasn't sure about any problems between the Volkovs and any other neighbors. Furthermore, he didn't think any of his neighbors would have or even could have been capable of the heinous crime.

As soon as the words had left Beanie's mouth, the name Rufus Mason entered his mind.

Supposedly, Mason had killed his wife, dismembered her, and buried her body beneath the mango tree in his backyard, but that was a rumor, origin unknown.

Strangely, Joshua Howard had occurred to him, but Beanie couldn't fathom his intern as a murder suspect. The idea of Joshua killing Ivan Volkov was as ridiculous as the thought of Natalya biting off Joshua's finger.

But, then again, maybe it wasn't so crazy. If Joshua and the Volkovs had some connection, then maybe the relationship had gone completely sideways, leading to dismemberment and death.

Beanie scoffed under his breath. He cautioned himself not to jump to unfounded conclusions. He needed to determine if, in fact, the intern and the Russian couple had a relationship before he declared their connection contentious or deadly.

Before leaving the crime scene, Beanie and Stevie managed to get a few abrasive, clipped comments from the detectives who arrived on the scene. Back at the *Palmchat Gazette* offices, Beanie and Stevie debriefed Vivian then collaborated for the next few hours on the story, which was made available on the paper's website an hour after it was filed, reviewed, edited, and revised. Minutes later, HIKERS FIND MANGLED CORPSE IN JUNGLE was trending as the *Palmchat Gazette's* most-read story.

Noelle shook her head and stood. "I think I need a beer."

"Bring me one too, please, babe," requested Beanie, pushing the mug of cold hot chocolate toward the centerpiece.

Back at the table, Noelle asked, "What do the cops think happened to Volkov?"

"He was stabbed in the chest," said Beanie, opening his beer. "The hikers who found him said he was lying on his stomach, and they turned the body over, hoping to help him by giving him CPR. They didn't know he was dead. They found the knife beneath his body. As for how his body got all ripped apart and chewed up—"

"Chewed up?" Noelle shuddered.

Beanie said, "It was pretty gruesome. There were dozens of bite wounds, some of them to the bone, all over Volkov's limbs and extremities."

Noelle shivered, tipped the beer bottle against her lips, tilted her head back, and took a long sip of the famous island brew. "Any idea who stabbed him?"

"None whatsoever," said Beanie. "When the cops questioned me about knowing Volkov, I realized that I didn't really know him."

Peeling a strip of the label from the beer bottle, Noelle said, "You don't think..."

"What?" Beanie peered at his wife.

Shaking her head, Noelle sighed. "Nothing."

"Tell me," Beanie prompted.

"It's dumb," said Noelle, waving a hand dismissively. "And ridiculous. And..."

"Do I think Natalya Volkov killed her husband?" asked Beanie, discerning what was on his wife's mind.

Noelle glanced at Beanie. "Well, we know she didn't because Ivan Volkov was stabbed and Natalya..."

"Natalya...what?" asked Beanie. "Were you about to say that Natalya would have attacked Volkov and eaten him?"

"That's not what I was going to say," insisted Noelle, looking sheepish.

"Babe, I thought the same thing," confessed Beanie. "When I saw Volkov's body, I thought Natalya had ripped him apart, and if I didn't know he'd been stabbed, I would still think that because..."

"Because some part of you wonders if the woman is a human eating shapeshifter?"

Beanie sighed, took another sip of beer. "But I know that's not true."

Noelle said, "Of course not, but Volkov was strange, not that I mean to speak ill of the dead, because I don't, and his wife is also odd, so it's easy to let your imagination run rampant."

"Speaking of letting my imagination run rampant," said Beanie, drumming his fingers against the glass bottle. "You know, for a moment, I thought Rufus Mason might have done it."

"Rufus Mason?" Noelle frowned. "Why would he kill Ivan Volkov?"

"People think Mason killed his wife, dismembered her and buried her in the backyard," said Beanie, then he took another sip of beer.

Noelle gave him a look. "Roland, you're always telling me that a suspect needs a motive, right? So, what's Mason's motive for killing Volkov?"

Beanie exhaled. "I only entertained that theory for a moment, until I realized that Mason has no motive to kill Volkov. I mean, Mason doesn't have a motive that I know about."

"Which doesn't mean that Mason *doesn't* have a motive." Noelle finished her beer. "But what if he does?"

"If so, then what could it be?" asked Beanie. "I'm not sure Mason even knows the Volkovs."

Noelle said, "He hardly leaves his house. Every now and then, I see him at the mailbox, and he barely says hello. Although, the last time I saw him, he mumbled a few words. But we weren't in the neighborhood. I saw him at the Coral House Nursery."

"What were you doing at Coral House Nursery?" asked Beanie.

"Mom and I were looking at roses," said Noelle. "Anyway, Mason was buying a white hibiscus plant, and we made polite conversation."

"Why was Mason buying a white hibiscus plant?"

Noelle shrugged. "Who knows? I didn't ask."

Beanie asked, "Did you and your mom buy any roses?"

Shaking her head, Noelle said, "No, we didn't. Mom said the petals looked brittle. Anyway, so, now that Ivan Volkov is dead, I'm assuming you're going to focus on that story, right?"

"Me and Stevie," said Beanie. "Talk about a dynamic duo, huh?"

Noelle scooped up the strips of the label she'd peeled from the bottle. "Listen, I know Ivan's story is important, and it'll probably be great for your brand, but don't forget about Joshua, okay? He's still missing."

"I know, which is very concerning and confusing," said Beanie. "Even more so since I found out his finger was bitten off. Bothers me that no one can reach him, and he's not returning any calls or texts."

"Do the police have any leads?" asked Noelle.

Beanie rubbed his jaw. "Last time I checked with Fields, he said the cops are still getting calls from people claiming to have seen Joshua, but none of the leads have been viable."

"Finding Joshua is important," said Noelle. "So don't stop looking for him."

Beanie finished his beer. "Believe me, I'm not. Since Fields told me that it was Joshua's finger we found in Ethan's candy pail, I can't help being worried. I've tried to think about it rationally. Logically."

"There's nothing logical or rational about biting someone's finger off."

Nodding, Beanie said, "Which is why I'm worried. And I want to find him. Make sure he's okay. Make sure he's not ..."

"Not what?"

Shaking his head, Beanie said, "I don't want to jump to conclusions or give into wild speculations like Friday, but what if she's right?"

"You mean, what if someone killed Joshua and cut him into little pieces?"

"No, no, I don't think that." Beanie reached across the table and grabbed Noelle's hand. "But Ivan Volkov's death rattled me. Makes me wonder ... I don't know. Crazy stuff. The point is, I just hope Joshua is found soon."

"What crazy stuff does Ivan's death make you wonder?" questioned Noelle.

Squeezing his wife's hands, Beanie sighed. "Ivan Volkov was bitten. Joshua's finger was bitten off. Again, I don't want to jump to conclusions, but I can't help wondering if there's a connection between the two crimes. Did the same person bite off Joshua's finger and kill Ivan Volkov?"

12

"The cops aren't going to tell us anything about the case," announced Beanie, sipping from his third cup of coffee as he walked into Stevie's cubicle.

"Why am I not surprised?" Stevie balled up a sheet of paper and lobbed it toward the mini basketball hoop mounted over the five-foot cubicle wall across from his desk.

Two days had passed since Ivan Volkov's body was found in the jungle on the east side of the island. Beanie had left dozens of messages for the detectives assigned to the case since then. Still, when his calls were returned, the police resolutely refused to provide additional comments about the progress of the investigation.

Beanie and Stevie had been reduced to designing infographics detailing the timeline of events surrounding Ivan Volkov's murder and publishing unsubstantiated accounts from several of Beanie's Oyster Farms neighbors. Mr. Mendez, of course, had given Beanie an earful of foolishness, most of it centered around his belief that Natalya Volkov had stabbed her husband, then morphed into a Siberian husky to eat the flesh from his bones.

"We're going to have to dig for information on our own," said Beanie.

"Why do the cops have to be so secretive?" asked Stevie, creating another paper ball. "What's the deal with giving us a comment? The public has a right to know if some murderous fiend is stalking the island, stabbing victims, and tearing them apart."

"I agree," said Beanie, nodding as he held up a hand to block the paper ball Stevie aimed at the basketball hoop.

"It's in the interest of public safety," said Stevie, grabbing another sheet of paper. "Their refusal to help us inform people is a dereliction of their duties as officers of the law."

"I hear you." Beanie blocked another paper ball, preventing its arc into the mini hoop.

Frowning, Stevie made another paper ball. "They're not protecting or serving by withholding information."

Beanie batted the paper ball to the speckled tile floor.

"Dude, stop blocking my shots," complained Stevie, scowling. "I'm trying to relieve stress."

What stress, thought Beanie, who still had problems wrapping his head around the fact that Stevie's family owned the Felipe Beer Company.

"Cops can be difficult," said Beanie, deciding not to block the next paper ball Stevie tossed at the mini hoop—and missed. "But they don't have to tell us anything, and they're not. Nevertheless, Vivian wants a follow-up with some facts and substantiated evidence, so I think we need to investigate Ivan Volkov. Let's find out more about him. Maybe there's something in his past that led to his murder."

A few hours later, following a quick lunch delivered from a local Indian restaurant, Beanie convened with Stevie in Vivian's office to tell the Managing Editor what they'd discovered.

"It's quite interesting," began Beanie, sitting next to Stevie in one of the two chairs positioned in front of Vivian's large desk. "Turns out, Ivan Volkov and his wife used to live in the Aerie Islands. They moved to St. Killian a year ago and took up residence on Dolphin Lane."

"They were renting the house," interjected Stevie, looking down at his phone. "It's owned by one of Beanie's neighbors. A child psychologist named Dr. Walter Zeller."

Beanie gave Stevie the side-eye. He hadn't expected Stevie to hijack his telling of the details they'd uncovered about the Volkovs. Beanie had planned to present the information in a more linear fashion. Stevie's style was more haphazard. He often emphasized details that weren't very important, like the Volkovs renting Zeller's house. Beanie planned to share that detail, but there were more interesting details to divulge first.

"Did Dr. Zeller know the Volkovs before they moved to St. Killian?" asked Vivian, grabbing a red pen from the coffee mug she used to hold writing instruments.

"Not sure," said Beanie. "But Dr. Zeller is on my list to interview."

"And another thing," said Stevie, "is that the Volkovs had lots of lawsuits filed against them while they lived in the Aerie Islands. A whole bunch of people pressed charges against them."

"Our research showed that Natalya Volkov was arrested for attacking and biting people more than two dozen times," said Beanie, feeling the need to take back the telling of the details, even though it made him feel unnecessarily competitive. "The attacks always occurred at night, and Ivan Volkov always blamed the attacks on their Siberian husky."

Vivian tapped the red pen against her lips. "Was there any proof that Natalya was biting people?"

Beanie said, "Not really. At the time of the attacks, Natalya was always out walking the dog. The people who claimed she attacked them reported the dog lunging at them. The dog would attack. Natalya would try to lure the dog away from them, and then they would be bitten when they weren't looking, but all of the victims reported that the teeth felt like human teeth."

"Were any of the bites tested for human saliva?" asked Vivian.

"Most of the tests came back inconclusive," said Stevie. "A lot of times, the victims would go to the hospital before they called the police, so there wasn't much physical evidence."

"But bites marks can be measured when they break the skin," said Vivian. "It's not hard to tell a human bite from an animal bite."

Beanie nodded. "Well, most of the cases didn't get very far because Ivan Volkov would offer to pay medical bills, so quite a few victims dropped the charges."

Vivian leaned back in her chair. "That is interesting, but I doubt any of those bite victims wanted revenge on Ivan Volkov. You think any of them were so angry they were bitten by his dog, or his wife, that they decided to kill him?"

Beanie shook his head. When he'd discovered the police reports against Natalya, he'd known the victims probably wouldn't be considered suspects. The victims had been compensated, which lessened the likelihood that one of them would target Volkov.

Stevie said, "But, there is evidence that maybe Natalya Volkov killed her husband."

Frowning, Beanie stared at Stevie. "What evidence?"

"A few months before the Volkovs left the Aerie Islands," said Stevie. "There were several domestic disturbances called in to the police by several of their neighbors."

"Domestic disturbances?" demanded Beanie. "What are you talking about?"

"While you were at lunch," said Stevie, "I researched a few more cases. The ones not related to dog bites."

"Is that so?" asked Beanie, trying to temper his frustration—and the niggling envy, which bothered him. Jealousy was counterproductive, Beanie knew, but he couldn't help feeling miffed that Stevie had kept crucial information from him. He also couldn't help wondering if Stevie had withheld the information on purpose, to impress Vivian, to make himself look like a better investigator.

"Tell me more about the domestic disturbances," requested Vivian, leaning forward, focused on Stevie.

"Neighbors reported hearing loud arguments," began Stevie. "But, the Volkovs always argued in Russian, so no one knew what they were saying. Other neighbors told the cops they frequently saw Ivan Volkov with scratches and bruises on his face and arms. Ivan Volkov told one of the neighbors he'd been mugged, but I couldn't find any police reports of an assault against him."

"The wife as a suspect is much more interesting than a few dog bite victims," said Vivian.

Beanie fought a burgeoning sense of inadequacy and betrayal. He and Stevie were supposed to be partners on the story. Beanie hoped Stevie wasn't angling for a solo byline, but if the brewery heir thought he could usurp Beanie and get away with it, he had another thing coming. Beanie was prepared to fight for the story. He considered Stevie a friend, but he had a mortgage to pay, a wife, and two growing boys to support. He didn't have a billionaire family to hand him whatever he needed on a platinum platter.

"Have either of you interviewed Natalya Volkov?" asked Vivian.

Beanie squirmed as the inadequate feelings intensified. Interviewing Volkov's wife should have been at the top of his list after the man was found dead. Why hadn't he? Maybe because Natalya Volkov was grieving, and he hadn't wanted to add to her misery with questions she probably would have refused to answer. Still, he couldn't sacrifice competency for compassion.

Stevie said, "Maybe Beanie should talk to Mrs. Volkov. He knows her. She's his neighbor. She'd probably be willing to answer his questions."

Vivian said, "I think that's a good idea."

Back at his desk, Beanie felt horrible for allowing his envy to run rampant and entertaining jealous thoughts about Stevie. Awful enough to call his twin sister, Robyn, and burden her with his guilt. The only person who truly understood his motives, fears, hopes, and negative tendencies was the person who had survived nine months in the womb with him.

"Don't beat yourself up, baby bro," said Robyn, using a nickname she often employed to remind him that she was seven minutes older than him. "Envy is a basic human emotion that we all fall prey to from time to time, but the fact that you just acknowledged the jealousy and didn't act on it proves that you have a good heart."

"Yeah, big sis, if you say so," said Beanie, pulling out a desk drawer and grabbing a small stress ball. Robyn was right, of course, but Beanie didn't like the competitiveness that had overtaken him when he thought Stevie had bested him.

"Makes sense that you're annoyed about sharing a story with a guy who's not the greatest reporter and to add insult to injury, doesn't even need the job. Then it seems like he's doing the most and doing it better than you, so of course, you feel some kind of way about it," said Robyn. "But I get the feeling you're upset about something other than Stevie stealing your thunder."

"You know me too well," Beanie admitted, smiling to himself as he dropped the stress ball back into the drawer. He didn't need a rubber ball to feel better when he had Robyn on his side, encouraging and supporting him. Reading his mind.

"You're worried about Joshua, aren't you?" asked Robyn.

"I'm trying not to, but it's hard," said Beanie. "And since Ivan Volkov was killed—"

"He was your strange neighbor, right?"

"One of my many strange neighbors," said Beanie, thinking of Mendez, Old Wilson, and Rufus Mason. "Anyway, I think Joshua knew the Volkovs, and now that Ivan is dead, I'm wondering if Joshua might be in danger."

"You think Joshua's in danger because he knew the Volkovs?"

"It's a little more complicated," explained Beanie, then went on to tell his sister about Joshua's trips to the Volkov house, including the two times he'd gone to their home on October 29th. "I think the Volkovs were the last people to see Joshua the day he disappeared."

"But you don't know the reason for these visits between the three of them," said Robyn.

"There was some sort of relationship," said Beanie. "But what was the nature of it?"

"I'd say it was pretty contentious," said Robyn. "I mean, considering that Ivan Volkov is dead, and Joshua's finger was bitten off."

Beanie rubbed his jaw. "I'm inclined to agree. But before I jump to conclusions, I need to find out more about the relationship."

"You're going to interview Natalya Volkov," said Robyn. "You should ask her."

"I plan to," said Beanie. "But will she tell me? Don't know, but I doubt it …"

13

An hour later, face to face with Natalya Volkov, Beanie stood in the small foyer, thanking her for agreeing to answer a few of his questions.

"We can talk in living room, yes?" asked the widow, avoiding Beanie's eyes as she gestured toward the room off the foyer with a pale, bony hand.

"That's fine," said Beanie, following Natalya into a space that was furnished with bamboo pieces and neutral colors, sandy shades that somehow weren't as bright and airy as they should have been. "We can talk wherever you feel comfortable."

Natalya sat on the edge of one of the four chairs grouped around a round wicker coffee table. She was dressed in a white T-shirt, jeans, and a beige cardigan that drowned her birdlike frame, accentuated her pallid complexion, and made her ice blue eyes look unnatural. Hunched forward, her shoulders drawn toward her chest, she wrapped her arms around her waist, as though seeking warmth.

"First of all," began Beanie, taking a seat in the chair next to her. "I want to say that I'm sorry about the passing of your husband."

Bringing a thin, trembling hand to her face, she sniffed and rubbed her nose. "Thank you."

"How have you been?" asked Beanie. "I can't imagine how hard this has been for you."

"It has been most horrible thing," said Natalya. "Ivan was love of my life. I cannot believe I will not see him again. Grow old with him. It is very hard to deal with. I am not sure how I will make it through, but I know I must."

Feeling sorry for the widow, Beanie asked, "Do you have any family who can come and be with you?"

Natalya shook her head and looked at the floor. "There is no one. For me, there was only Ivan, and now he is gone. It is even worse because he did not die by disease or old age, but he was killed in such horrible way. The police said he was stabbed, and his body was torn apart like by wild animal. So, so terrible. It breaks my heart how he must have suffered."

Beanie's heart went out to the woman. Despite her bizarre behavior and strange demeanor, he knew her grief was real and raw. "Mrs. Volkov—"

"What is worse is police," said Natalya, staring at him with those ice-blue eyes. "They are not kind."

"What do you mean?" asked Beanie, recognizing his opening to question the widow.

"They ask me so many questions," said Natalya, shaking her head, clasping her shaking hands. "Over and over. They try to make me say I hurt Ivan, but I never would. I never could hurt Ivan. He was love of my life!"

Nodding, Beanie said, "What did the police ask you?"

"They want to know where I was when Ivan was killed," said Natalya. "They want to know everything Ivan did the day he died. They want so many details. They want to know things I do not know. Things I can't remember. They do not believe me. They think I am not telling the truth! They do not understand!"

"What don't they understand?" asked Beanie, concerned by Natalya's trembling shoulders as she swayed from side to side.

"They do not understand," said Natalya, her ice-blue eyes wide and wild. "It is in my blood!"

Confused, Beanie asked, "What do you mean? What's in your blood?"

"The sickness!" shouted Natalya, rocking back and forth with increasing velocity. "It is in my blood! It has always been from the time I was a small child! I have always had the sickness. I tried to explain, but the police do not believe me! It is in my blood, in my soul! There is no hope for me, no hope!"

"Mrs. Volkov, please," said Beanie, his apprehension growing. "Try to calm down. Please. I didn't mean to upset you."

"The police are not kind," said Natalya, rubbing her hands up and down her splotchy red cheeks. "They think I hurt Ivan, but I could never do that! Ivan was love of my life!"

"Mrs. Volkov," said Beanie, feeling as though he shouldn't make any sudden moves as the widow grew more agitated. "Do you know who might have wanted to kill your husband?"

"Mr. Mendez thinks I killed Ivan," said Natalya, rocking more vehemently. "He said things to me that are not kind! He says he will prove I am a killer, but he is wrong! I loved Ivan! He was the only one who believed the sickness could be cured! I could never hurt him! I could ... I don't ... I ..."

"Mrs. Volkov?" Beanie stood. "Are you okay?"

Natalya Volkov's body went rigid, her head snapping back and forth. Red splatters bruised her pale skin as her lips shrank back into a snarl, revealing straight, white teeth.

Panic flooded Beanie, racing through him.

Glaring at Beanie, her ice-blue eyes glittering, Natalya Volkov growled, the sound like a gargled scream as she stood and turned to him.

"Mrs. Volkov," whispered Beanie, keeping one eye on the widow, and the other toward the foyer, trying to judge the distance. "Please try to calm down, okay? I'm sorry I upset you, but—"

With a primal snarl, Natalya lunged at Beanie, jumping at him with her hands curled into claws. Shocked and caught off guard, Beanie raised his hands, trying to defend himself, but the widow slammed into him. Losing his footing, Beanie fought to stay on his feet, but he lost his balance. Beanie fell backward, crashing down onto the coffee table, and then rolling to the floor. Natalya crawled on top of him, snarling, her teeth bared. His heart pounding, Beanie grabbed Natalya's wrists, wrestling with the widow, struggling to get the crazed woman off him. What was happening? Was this real? Beanie didn't know what to think. His mind was blank. Every instinct diverted toward a plan of escape.

Natalya continued to snarl, snapping her teeth as she tried to lower her head. Was she trying to bite him? Crazy thoughts infected Beanie's mind.

Had Mr. Mendez been right about the widow? Was she about to shapeshift into a Siberian husky? No, that was crazy! Ridiculous. Beanie didn't have time to entertain foolishness!

He had to get Natalya off him. But how? She was strong. Her thin limbs were more powerful than they appeared as she fought to free herself from his grasp. Beanie didn't want to hurt the woman, but—

Loud, guttural barks seized Beanie's heart.

Natalya screamed and pulled away from Beanie. Rolling across the floor, she jumped to her feet as the Siberian husky – the same ice-blue eyed dog that had twice lunged at Beanie – ran up to her, barking fiercely.

Confused, Beanie sat up and scooted back.

"No, please, no!" she shouted, sobbing hysterically while the dog continued to bark. "Stop! Stop!"

Beanie rose slowly.

Natalya expelled a long, plaintive wail and then collapsed, her body seizing.

The husky turned its large head toward Beanie, fixing him with its ice-blue eyes.

"Easy, boy … easy …" said Beanie, feeling as though he'd gone from the frying pan into the fire.

As the dog moved back to Natalya and lowered itself to the floor, lying next to her, Beanie carefully removed his phone from his pocket and called 911.

14

"I can't believe Natalya attacked you," said Noelle, on her knees in the king-sized bed, fluffing the pillow before Beanie eased back and let his head sink into the soft goose down.

"Neither can I," said Beanie, though he'd experienced and survived Natalya Volkov's vicious assault. "Couldn't even believe it was happening. It was so ... surreal."

Surreal was an understatement. Hours later, Natalya's unprovoked attack still had him shaken, reeling from memories of her growling and snapping teeth.

"She's a batcrap psycho," Noelle fumed. "And she should be in jail. I can't believe they didn't arrest her for attempted murder.

As his wife stretched out on the bed next to him, Beanie sighed. "Well, there was no proof that she attacked me."

"No proof?"

"She *didn't* bite me, Elle," reminded Beanie.

"Only because you were able to get away from her," said Noelle.

"Actually, I think the dog saved my life," said Beanie, recalling the husky's commanding barks and Natalya's immediate Pavlovian response.

"Too bad the dog can't give a statement to the police," groused Noelle.

Beanie chuckled. "Don't think anyone at St. K.P.D. speaks 'bark.'"

"That's not funny, Roland," said Noelle, though she gave him a small smile.

"The cops took Natalya down to the station and questioned her," said Beanie. "But it came down to my word against hers. And there was no physical evidence. Fields said I could press charges, but I figured why bother? How would I prove what she did?"

"When the police talked to her, what did she have to say for herself?" asked Noelle. "Although I can't imagine how she could explain what she did to you or why."

"I asked Fields when he called a few hours ago, and he said she didn't say much," said Beanie. "He says she was almost catatonic."

Noelle scoffed. "Convenient."

"He said she claimed to have no memory of attacking me," said Beanie.

"Why am I not surprised?" asked Noelle. "I hope the police saw through her lies. She's violent and dangerous."

Nodding, Beanie said, "I agree. The way she came at me ... she was so ferocious. Like an animal. Babe, I think Old Wilson was telling the truth. I didn't at first, but now I think she bit him."

"He wasn't the only person she bit," said Noelle. "Remember all those people in the Aerie Islands she attacked? And then she and Ivan paid them off so they wouldn't tell the truth about her."

Rubbing his jaw, Beanie glanced at the ceiling fan, swirling lazily above them. "I think she killed Ivan, too."

"You do?"

Glancing at his wife, Beanie said, "Stevie did some research on the Volkovs and found out about some domestic disturbances that occurred when they lived in the Aerie Islands. Apparently, neighbors heard the Volkovs arguing a lot, and Ivan was seen covered in scratches and bruises several times."

Noelle's eyes widened. "Covered in scratches and bruises?"

Beanie said, "Ivan claimed he'd been mugged, but I'm convinced that Natalya must have attacked him. Must have come at him the same way she came at me."

"Like a wolf," said Noelle.

"Like a crazed psychopath," said Beanie. "Ivan's corpse had bite marks all over it. Natalya must have bitten him. She attacked him, tore him apart, and … what I can't figure out is why? What's her motive?"

"Psychopaths don't really need a motive, do they?"

"Before she lunged at me, she said something about a sickness in her blood," said Beanie.

"So she knows she's crazy," said Noelle.

"Maybe. Maybe not," said Beanie. "But, it makes me wonder if she goes into some sort of trance and kills in a blind rage and then comes out of the trance with no memory."

Noelle sighed. "I suppose that's possible."

"You know what else I think is possible?" asked Beanie, a sliver of sly apprehension washing over him. "That she bit off Joshua's finger. I think it happened the night he went to see the Volkovs. After Friday dropped him off in Oyster Farms. Whatever their relationship is, or was, it got violent that night. Natalya attacked Joshua, bit his finger off, and then …"

"And then … what do you think happened?"

"That's what I don't know," said Beanie. "I just hope that, someway, Joshua got out of that house. Wherever he is, I hope he's okay."

15

"Palmito?" offered Florence Taylor as she extended a tall, frosty glass of the island's official drink toward Beanie.

"I shouldn't," said Beanie, taking a seat on the large sectional couch in the outdoor living room of the enormous covered terrace. "I'm still on the clock."

Making a face, Florence said, "That's too bad."

"You sure?" asked Florence's husband, Chuck Taylor, who lounged on an oversized chaise across from the couch.

"Another time," said Beanie, shifting his gaze from Chuck, who resembled a cooked lobster right out of the pot, red and sweaty. Taking in the lush, tropical landscaping of the Taylor's huge backyard, Beanie reminded himself not to be envious of the couple's million-dollar abode. Their neighborhood, Avalon Estates, was aspirational, with its wide, palm-lined avenues and giant mansions, but the residents lived a lifestyle of the rich and shameless.

"You don't know what you're missing," said Chuck. "Flo only uses the best rum for her Palmitos. Bishop's Reserve."

Beanie couldn't help but be impressed. Bishop's Reserve, considered the best rum in the world, was extremely expensive. The premier rum was distilled by the Bishop family, who owned the Felipe Brewery. A bottle of the rare, highly prized rum would set a person back thousands of dollars. Even though Stevie Bishop, Beanie's coworker, was a scion of the billionaire family, Beanie had never had a sip of Bishop's Reserve. He wanted to taste the superior libation, but not at a quarter after nine in the morning. It was definitely too early for rum, even Bishop's Reserve, but he doubted the Taylors felt the same way.

Clearing his throat, Beanie said, "So you have some information for me?"

When Beanie had arrived at work, Millie, the receptionist, informed him about an important message from someone who claimed to have urgent information about Joshua Howard. Information Beanie needed to know. The caller's contact information, Millie had told him, was in his email inbox.

In his cubicle, Beanie powered up his computer and then walked to the break room for his first cup of coffee. He was curious about the caller and the information, but also cautious. Beanie wasn't in the mood to get excited about a lead to nowhere. The police had been inundated with false sightings. Hundreds of residents had sworn they'd seen the intern, and the cops had investigated each lead, but so far, Joshua was still missing.

Back at his desk, he'd checked his email.

The message from Chuck and Florence Taylor filled him with annoyance. He'd met the ex-pats at an Easter egg hunt outing earlier in the year during which the host's wife had been found dead. Beanie wasn't too keen on the couple, who were rich, well-traveled, and filled with schadenfreude.

"Not just information," said Chuck, after a healthy gulp of his drink. "We have explosive revelations."

"You will never believe what we found out," said Florence as she on the L-shaped section of the couch.

"Well, don't keep me in suspense," said Beanie, though he doubted what they planned to tell him was explosive or unbelievable.

Florence took a long sip of her Palmito, then said, "Well, as we wrote to you in our message, the information concerns the missing student, Joshua Harris."

"Howard," corrected Beanie.

Florence frowned. "I'm sorry."

"His name is Joshua Howard," said Beanie.

"Are you sure?" questioned Florence, slight suspicion in her bleary gaze. "I could have sworn I read Joshua Harris."

"Well, I'm sure I wrote Joshua Howard," said Beanie. "Because that's his name."

Florence gave him a dubious look, then shrugged and said, "Well, anyway, as Chuck said, we have an explosive revelation."

"Okay, let's hear it," said Beanie, nodding. Driving to the couple's palatial estate, Beanie pondered what information Chuck and Florence might have about Joshua. Beanie couldn't imagine that the intern would have anything in common with a snarky, wealthy couple. He doubted they traveled in the same social circles or knew any of the same people. Turning into the Taylor's circular driveway, Beanie had reminded himself that he wouldn't have guessed that Joshua had a connection to a bizarre Russian couple, but ...

But, actually, Beanie still hadn't confirmed a relationship between Joshua and the Volkovs. He suspected Joshua had walked to the Volkov house after his shift on October 29th, but he didn't know that for sure. He had no proof, only gut instinct.

Standing, Florence said, "Let me make myself another drink first."

"Make me another, too," requested Chuck.

Beanie resisted the urge to groan.

Ten minutes later, with fresh Palmitos, the Taylors were ready to disseminate their explosive news.

"Yesterday, I was talking to Rosa, one of our housekeepers, about the linen rotation schedule for the guest bedrooms," began Florence, "and she seemed distracted, so I asked her what was on her mind, she told me she was upset with her daughter. So, of course, I asked her why."

Of course, thought Beanie. He doubted Florence would ever pass up the chance to collect a potentially juicy tidbit of gossip.

Chuck said, "Rosa told Flo that her daughter had some information about the missing boy in the paper, meaning Joshua Howard, but her daughter didn't want to go to the police."

"Rosa's daughter recognized Joshua," said Florence. "The daughter works for a lawyer, but he's one of those shady ambulance chasers. Not reputable at all."

"Not board-certified, either," said Chuck, who was nearly finished with his second Palmito.

"Anyway," said Florence. "Rosa said that, according to her daughter, Joshua hired the shady lawyer because he wanted to sue some Russian couple."

Chuck said, "Turns out, it's the same Russian couple you've been writing about."

"The man who was found dead in the jungle," said Florence. "And his bizarre wife who attacked you. Isn't that something?"

"I have a feeling it is," said Beanie, recalling the story he'd written about his attempt to interview Natalya Volkov. The woman's unexplained violence had been chronicled in the article, *WIFE DENIES INVOLVEMENT IN JUNGLE CORPSE MURDER*, written with Stevie's assistance the day after Natalya had attacked Beanie. Together, he and Stevie had provided a detailed account of the accusations against Natalya from their research into her life in the Aerie Islands. They'd outlined Natalya's vehement denial of any involvement in her husband's murder, providing a play-by-play of Beanie's impromptu interview with the widow, which seemed to have been the impetus for her rage against him.

"Flo, tell him about the mediation where the wife went batcrap crazy," said Chuck.

"What mediation?" asked Beanie.

Her tone conspiratorial, Florence said, "Apparently, the shady lawyer hired a mediator to help the two parties—one being Joshua and the other the Russian couple—reach a settlement agreement. Rosa's daughter told Rosa that the mediation didn't go well."

"The wife had some sort of attack," said Chuck, a hint of malicious glee in his gaze.

"An attack," echoed Beanie, apprehension washing over him as flashes of Natalya's growling, teeth snapping flooded his mind, mixing with images of Ivan's horrible corpse and the finger in Ethan's candy pail.

"The wife broke out in hives, according to Rosa's daughter," said Florence, excitement alight in her eyes. "And then the wife started growling.

Rosa said it was terrifying. The wife started snapping her teeth and lunging at Joshua—just like what happened to you! Isn't that bizarre?"

His apprehension turning to dread, Beanie stared at Florence.

"Rosa's daughter thinks it was some kind of seizure," said Chuck. "They offered to call an ambulance, but the husband declined and got the wife out of there as fast as he could."

"Isn't that awful?" asked Florence, sounding more delighted than disturbed. "That poor woman needed medical attention, so why did the husband refuse help? That's what I wonder. That's what I find suspicious. It's like he didn't want his wife to go to the hospital. But why? Did he not want the doctors to treat her? And if so, why not?"

Because he didn't want the doctors to find out that his wife was a homicidal maniac, thought Beanie. A woman prone to unprovoked, uncontrollable rage, and violent hostility against others. A woman who'd attacked before, leaving her victims battered and bruised, and most likely, confused.

"You know what I think?" slurred Chuck. "Drugs. I'll bet the wife was starting to OD. Probably took some bath salts."

"Oh, Chuck, I'll bet you're right," said Florence. "Bath salts make people crazy. Remember that guy in Florida who thought he was a zombie? Didn't he bite someone?"

Clearing his throat, Beanie said, "You mentioned that Rosa was upset with her daughter for not going to the cops. What did Rosa think her daughter could tell the police?"

"Well, after the first failed mediation," said Florence. "Rosa's daughter called the Russians to set up a meeting to discuss another mediation. She spoke to the wife, who told her that Joshua was an evil person who would get what he deserved, which was to die. Now that Joshua is missing, Rosa's daughter thinks the wife had something to do with Joshua's disappearance."

Chuck said, "Flo and I figure the crazy wife killed Joshua."

Disturbed by the ex-pat's unfounded speculation, Beanie said, "Joshua is not dead."

"Are you sure he's not?" asked Chuck, his gaze shrewd.

"Wasn't one of his toes found in a child's candy pail?" asked Flo.

"Joshua's finger was found in the candy pail," said Beanie, glad he'd decided not to publish that he'd found the finger.

Flo gave Beanie a suspicious look. "Could have sworn it was one of his toes."

Chuck said, "Question is, where is the rest of him?"

An hour later, back in his cubicle at the *Palmchat Gazette*, Beanie shared the Taylor's information with Stevie and Vivian, who decided that Beanie should craft an article for the paper's website. The story would focus on the connection between Joshua and the Volkovs. A few more hours later, *MISSING STUDENT SUED JUNGLE CORPSE* was trending. Several commenters wondered if Natalya Volkov knew anything about Joshua's disappearance. Many believed the police should question her in light of the new facts. Considering that Natalya had attacked Beanie, some speculated that she might have bitten Joshua's finger off. A few went so far as to raise the possibility that Natalya had killed her husband, Ivan.

Despite his dislike of the Taylors, Beanie was thankful the couple had exposed the connection between the intern and the Russian couple. Beanie finally had a valid reason for Joshua's visit to the Volkov house on October 29th before his shift ended. Joshua must have gone to see the Volkovs about the lawsuit. Maybe he went back to the peach-colored bungalow hoping to convince the couple to fulfill their promise to compensate him for the injuries he'd sustained when Natalya bit him. There had probably been an argument about the lawsuit. After being sued before and having to pay so many settlements, maybe the Volkovs decided they were tired of shelling out cash to victims. Or, perhaps, they didn't have the money to pay Joshua. The intern might have insisted on payment. Joshua's determination to be compensated might have enraged Natalya. Beanie figured the disagreement escalated into violence.

Leaning back in his chair, Beanie listened to the old, cracked leather creak. Natalya's attack at the mediation was further proof that the woman was violent and dangerous. If not for Ivan holding her back, Natalya might have attacked Joshua a second time. Beanie shuddered, remembering Natalya's violence against him. He wouldn't describe the woman's growling and teeth snapping as a seizure. And he doubted the woman had been about to have a seizure at the mediation. If Natalya had seizures, then Ivan Volkov would have insisted on calling paramedics, considering that seizures could be fatal.

Beanie sat forward. He needed to find out more about the lawsuit Joshua filed against the Volkovs.

Minutes later, after researching the St. Killian Civil Cases database, he located the petition to file the suit. Much like the lawsuits filed against the Volkovs in the Aerie Islands, Joshua's complaint painted Natalya as psychotic and homicidal. His petition claimed Natalya had attacked him without provocation. Apparently, Joshua had been picking up a package from the Volkov house when the door opened. Natalya accused Joshua of putting packages on her porch that didn't belong to her. As Joshua denied her accusations, Natalya lunged at him and bit his shoulder. The bite had been so severe that it punctured the fabric of Joshua's polo shirt, broke the skin, and required fourteen butterfly stitches.

As he printed a copy of the petition, Beanie realized that when he showed Natalya Volkov the photo of Joshua, she'd recognized him as the courier she'd attacked. He was the plaintiff from the disastrous mediation—where she'd broken out into hives and lunged at him. Joshua had sued Natalya and her husband, which she was obviously well aware of, but she probably wanted to keep it quiet. She and Ivan didn't want anyone to know about the previous lawsuits against them, considering they'd been sued because of Natalya's violence.

Beanie wondered about the details of the mediation between the Volkovs and Joshua. Had the Taylors told him the truth or had they embellished the events, making them more vicious and lurid? Had Natalya lunged at Joshua? Had she growled? Beanie could think of one person who might know the answer to his question.

16

"Natalya Volkov killed Joshua," insisted Friday, her left leg, crossed over the right, swinging from side to side like an out of control pendulum. "I know it."

Sitting on the stone bench next to Joshua's girlfriend, Beanie hoped his butt wouldn't go numb before he had the chance to question Friday about the lawsuit Joshua had filed against the Volkovs. Specifically, he wanted to know the details of the settlement between Joshua and the Volkovs. He figured Friday would know, so he'd called her.

Friday eagerly agreed to meet. She'd been hoping he would call, she told him, after reading that Joshua's finger had been bitten off. When Beanie met her in the library courtyard, she'd immediately waylaid him with her theory about Natalya.

"She bit Joshua's finger off, and then she killed him, which is what I told the cops. Well, I tried to tell them. I called them and left a message for the officer assigned to the missing person report I filed, but he ignored me. The cops never called me back. Can you believe that?"

Beanie sighed under his breath. What he couldn't believe was Friday's outfit. Once again, she looked as though a package of crayons had exploded all over her. For their impromptu afternoon meeting in the courtyard of the St. Killian library, she wore orange-rimmed glasses, fuchsia Capri pants, and a purple tank top. The platinum pompadour remained the same—sleek and stiff. The riot of colors had caught the attention of several tourists posing for photos in the picturesque setting, but if Friday noticed the curious stares aimed in her direction, she didn't seem to care.

"I think they didn't call back because there's no proof that Natalya bit Joshua's finger off," said Beanie. "And there's no proof that Joshua is dead."

"Just because there's no proof doesn't mean that Natalya didn't hurt Joshua," said Friday, her narrowed gaze suspicious.

"That's true," said Beanie. "And hopefully the cops will question her about Joshua, but if there's no proof that she did anything to him, the police aren't going to arrest her for a crime she may or may not have committed."

Friday's wildly swinging leg went still as she gaped at Beanie. "A crime she may or may not have committed? Are you serious? You of all people should know she's out of her mind. She attacked you, too. I read the article you wrote. She lunged at you and tried to bite you. I know she did the same thing to Joshua. She attacked him, but he didn't get away like you did. Natalya killed him, I know it."

Nodding, Beanie said, "Actually, I agree with you. I think Natalya attacked Joshua. And I'm inclined to believe that she killed her husband. But the police don't base their investigations on my speculations and inclinations. They want hard facts, and I don't have any to give them, so…"

"So the cops don't believe you, either." She scoffed, and her leg started to swing again, but not so chaotically. "Why am I not surprised? The cops didn't believe Iris, and now even her friend, the reporter, is starting to doubt her."

"Iris?" asked Beanie.

"The main character in *The Lost Husband*," said Friday, her tone suggesting she thought Beanie was daft, or out of touch. "Remember I told you I was reading that book when we first met."

Beanie asked, "You haven't finished it?"

"I'm halfway through it," said Friday.

"Hmmm…" said Beanie, wondering what she would think when she got to the jaw-dropping twist.

Friday said, "I would have been finished by now, but I'm so worried about Joshua that I can't concentrate."

Clearing his throat, Beanie said, "Listen, I don't want to take up too much of your time. I called because I wanted to ask you about the lawsuit Joshua filed against Natalya and Ivan Volkov."

Friday's eyes narrowed for a quick second, and then she looked away.

"You do know about the lawsuit, right?"

Pulling on the lobe of her right ear, she said, "Yeah, I know about it."

"Did Joshua tell you what happened at the mediation?" asked Beanie.

Glancing at him, Friday said, "He didn't have to tell me. I was at the mediation. Worst day ever. Joshua wouldn't budge on his demands. The Russians wouldn't concede to anything. Then Natalya starts turning every shade of red imaginable. Then she jumps up and tries to lunge at Joshua, but Ivan grabs her. By that time, Natalya is growling. The lawyer and his assistant think she's having some sort of medical emergency. I was convinced she was going to start foaming at the mouth. Ivan tells us she's okay, she just needs air. We tell him she needs an ambulance. He refuses. She keeps growling. At that point, Ivan hustles her out of the mediator's office."

"And then what?" asked Beanie.

"And then we all just sat there staring at each other," said Friday. "None of us could believe what had just happened. I'd never been so terrified and yet fascinated in my whole life. I don't know if it was horrifyingly odd. Or, oddly horrifying. Joshua and I argued about it for days. We almost broke up."

"Why did you argue about the mediation?" asked Beanie.

"Because I wanted him to drop the stupid lawsuit," said Friday. "Especially after what happened at the mediation. But that sleazy attorney didn't care that Natalya Volkov is psycho. He kept encouraging Joshua to do whatever it took to get the Volkovs to settle with him."

Beanie stared at Friday. "What did the lawyer mean when he said Joshua should do whatever it took?"

Friday expelled a heavy exhale. "After the mediation debacle, the lawyer told Joshua that he needed some leverage on the Volkovs. The lawyer said the Volkovs needed some motivation. Something that would force them to pay Joshua, and then he would drop the lawsuit."

"Did Joshua find leverage to motivate the Volkovs?" asked Beanie, thinking that the motivation sounded like blackmail.

"I'm not sure about that," said Friday. "But, I think so because Joshua started following Mr. Volkov, and he told me he'd found out the truth about his wife, and he was going to get a lot of money from them."

"What truth about Volkov's wife did he find out?"

Shaking her head, Friday said, "He wouldn't tell me. Just said Volkov was going to give him a lot of money to stay quiet. I think he decided to blackmail the Volkovs. I told him it was wrong. I told him those people were crazy and not to be messed with, but Joshua wouldn't listen to me. Now he's missing, and I'm getting really frantic. I know Natalya did something bad to Joshua. I know she killed him. Just like she killed her husband."

"Listen," began Beanie. "There is no proof that Joshua is dead, or that Natalya did anything bad to him."

"But it makes sense that she would kill him, doesn't it?" asked Friday. "If Joshua found out some secret about Natalya that she was trying to keep hidden, she might have tried to stop Joshua from revealing that secret."

As Friday's tone rose several octaves, Beanie cautioned himself not to feed her unfounded fears with his theories. The desperation in her gaze hinted at a full-scale meltdown. He feared she might become histrionic and hysterical.

"What if Joshua went back to the Volkovs and asked for more money?" asked Friday. "I've been thinking about who Joshua went to see in Oyster Farms that night I dropped him off at the neighborhood park, and I believe he went to see the Volkovs."

"To ask for money?"

Nodding, she said, "And the Russians didn't want to pay him. So, Joshua threatened to go public with the wife's secret, and then they ..."

"Listen, let's not jump to conclusions, okay," advised Beanie, disturbed by the logic in Friday's theory, which mirrored his own speculations. "Let me get more facts. I'll talk to my police sources and do some more digging."

"And if I need to panic, you'll let me know?"

"I'm sure it won't come to that." Beanie tried to give her a reassuring smile. "But, if it does, I'll let you know."

17

"Eat your eggs, bud," instructed Beanie, giving Ethan what he hoped was a warning glance.

Leaning against the sink, Beanie sipped coffee as his oldest son sat at the kitchen table, scowling at the fluffy scrambled eggs he pushed around his plate with a fork. Ethan had devoured the waffles, which he'd drenched in syrup, despite an admonishment from Noelle, and he'd polished off two goat sausage patties, but the eggs were proving to be a struggle.

"Do I have to, Daddy?" asked Ethan, his voice plaintive, but with hints of subtle manipulation. Beanie recognized the tone. Whenever Ethan didn't want to do something—like make his bed, or stop playing video games, or eat nutritious foods—he would affect the sweetest little, pitiful whine. Beanie tried not to fall for his son's machinations, but the tyke was so cute, with his big brown eyes. It was hard not to give in and let Ethan have his way.

"Yes, Ethan, you have to eat your eggs," said Noelle, strolling into the kitchen, holding Evan, who was dressed and ready for pre-school.

"Eat eggs!" echoed Evan, clapping his hands. "Eat Eggs!

"Your brother ate his eggs," Beanie pointed out. "You don't want a two-year-old to outdo you."

"Roland, don't encourage competition," said Noelle, passing Evan to him.

Placing his coffee mug on the counter, Beanie said, "I wasn't encouraging competition, I was just—"

"Ethan, here's the deal, little man," said Noelle. "You either eat the eggs, or you don't get any dessert tonight."

Negative reinforcement, thought Beanie, kissing Evan's chubby cheeks. He wasn't sure it would work, but he wasn't going to point that out to Noelle. For the most part, she was the better disciplinarian.

His gaze shrewd, Ethan asked, "What's for dessert?"

Beanie chuckled as Noelle threw up her hands and shook her head.

"Go and get dressed for school," ordered Noelle, grabbing the plate of cold, picked over eggs as Ethan, his grin triumphant, skipped out of the kitchen.

"Dress for school!" said Evan. "Dress for school."

"That kid of yours," said Noelle, scraping the uneaten eggs into the garbage disposal.

"That kid of mine?" asked Beanie as Evan laid his head against Beanie's shoulder.

Noelle faced him. "You spoil him. He's always testing the limits, trying to see what he can get away with, and he knows that he can get away with pretty much anything."

Beanie didn't want to believe her assessment was fair, but he had a feeling it was. "Well … he's a kid, Elle. That's what kids do. They try to get away with not doing what they don't want to do."

Folding her arms, Noelle said, "You should have backed me up about the eggs."

"Back up eggs," said Evan, giggled. "Daddy, back up eggs."

"You little parrot," said Beanie, tweaking Evan's nose.

Laughing, Evan pressed his little fingers against Beanie's nose.

"Roland …"

Recognizing the irritation in his wife's voice, Beanie said, "How about this? I'll back you up about the dessert."

"You promise?" asked Noelle, her gaze dubious.

"I promise," said Beanie.

"Because you know he's going to make a case for why he should have dessert even though he didn't finish his eggs," said his wife.

"He can be a tough little negotiator," said Beanie. "But we'll be ready."

"Ready for what, Daddy?" asked Ethan, skipping back into the kitchen, dressed in khaki Bermuda shorts and a polo shirt.

"Ready to go to school," said Beanie, ruffling Ethan's curly fauxhawk as he and Noelle shepherded him out of the kitchen.

Several hours later, working on his third cup of coffee, Beanie deleted unwanted emails from his inbox.

He should have been working on a follow-up piece about Ivan Volkov's horrific murder, which the paper had dubbed "The Jungle Corpse Murder," but there had been little movement in the case. The police had few leads, and what information they had obtained, they still weren't inclined to share it with the *Palmchat Gazette*.

Beanie leaned back in the leather chair and studied the water stains on the ceiling tiles.

His thoughts pivoted to the lawsuit Joshua had filed against the Volkovs. One particular detail confused him. Bothered him. Joshua claimed Natalya had attacked him because he'd put packages that didn't belong to the Volkovs on their porch. Didn't make sense. Why would he do that?

Maybe Joshua had delivered the packages to the wrong house. A simple mistake. A possible annoyance. But, certainly not a reason to attack the guy. To take a bite out of his shoulder. Again, Natalya's actions proved her vicious volatility. Despite the lack of proof, Beanie was even more convinced that Natalya had bitten off Joshua's finger.

Drumming his fingers against his desk, Beanie reflected on Joshua's failed mediation with the Volkovs. His thoughts meandered to Friday's confession that Joshua's lawyer had encouraged him to get leverage against Ivan and Natalya. And obviously Joshua had found something incriminating. Friday claimed that Joshua knew some secret about Natalya. What had Joshua found out? And had what he'd learned spurred Natalya to attack him?

Beanie pinched the bridge of his nose. He had no proof that Joshua had visited the Volkovs after his shift ended. No evidence that after Friday dropped him off in Oyster Farms, he'd walked to the Volkov house, but

Beanie believed he had. And at the Volkov's, he imagined that Joshua had revealed to the couple that he knew the secret they wanted to keep hidden. There must have been an argument. And then there was violence.

The theory was fascinating. Secrets and blackmail and threats were salacious details that could garner lots of clicks, and page reads, Beanie knew. The only problem was proving the theory. Beanie needed more than just rampant speculation. He needed facts. He needed evidence.

Beanie's desk phone rang, and he picked up the receiver. "Roland Bean."

Officer Damon Fields said, "Hey, you got a minute?"

"I got a few," said Beanie. "What's up?"

"I found out a few things you might be interested in knowing," said Fields.

"Always," said Beanie, eager for information.

"Things you didn't hear from me, of course," said Fields, voice lowered.

"Absolutely," agreed Beanie. Turning to his computer, he opened a Word file to make notes of the details Fields would give him.

"We lifted prints from the knife used to stab Volkov," said Fields. "Forensics is still trying to identify them. I'll let you know if we get a match."

"I appreciate that," said Beanie.

"Also, traces of human saliva were found in Volkov's bite wounds," said Officer Fields.

"So, someone bit him," said Beanie, his mind leaping to Natalya Volkov.

"We don't know who yet," said Fields. "Forensics teams are working on it."

"Since we're talking about Ivan Volkov," began Beanie. "Any suspects yet? Anyone you like for the murder?"

Fields said, "Again, between you and me…"

"Of course," promised Beanie, anxious to find out if the St. K.P.D. shared his suspicions of Natalya.

"We like the wife," said Fields. "No evidence against her, but as you know, she's attacked before. She's never killed before, we don't think, but there's always a first time for everything, right?"

"Listen, I was wondering," said Beanie. "Has Natalya been questioned about Joshua Howard? I know there's no proof that she had anything to do with his disappearance, but Joshua sued the Volkovs. And I think Natalya and Ivan might have been the last people to see Joshua on October 29th."

"We knew that Joshua's delivery truck was parked outside the Volkov house on October 29th," said Fields. "We talked to the owner of the delivery company and found out his truck had been parked outside their house several times before, so some detectives went to talk to Natalya. This was before her husband died. She didn't have much to say. Denied knowing Joshua. Claimed she'd never seen him before and didn't know why his truck had been parked in front of her house."

Beanie said, "When I talked to her about Joshua—"

"She attacked you."

"Actually, she attacked me the second time I went to interview her," said Beanie. "That was after Ivan was murdered. The first time I talked to her, I asked her about Joshua. She denied knowing him or recognizing him, but I knew she was lying. I think she attacked him. Bit his finger off."

"Well, we got a DNA sample when she came to the station after you said she attacked you," said Fields. "If she bit Joshua, we'll be able to prove it."

18

"Fields just called with some very interesting information," Beanie told Stevie, who'd drifted into Beanie's cubicle moments ago.

"What did he tell you?" asked Stevie, dressed in ratty board shorts and a T-shirt, looking more like a beach bum than the scion of a billionaire family.

"Yesterday, my neighbor, Mr. Mendez, showed up at the police station claiming to have proof that Natalya Volkov had something to do with Joshua's disappearance."

"What kind of proof?" asked Stevie, consulting his phone as he slouched in the chair across from the desk in Beanie's small cubicle.

"Mendez has a video that shows Joshua going into the Volkov house at 9:32 p.m. on October 29th," Beanie said, taking a sip of lukewarm coffee. "But Joshua does not come out of the house."

"Did the police talk to Natalya about Mendez's video?" asked Stevie.

Leaning back in his chair, Beanie said, "Fields said they couldn't get anything out of her. She claims not to remember Joshua coming to her house that day. She said she didn't know who Joshua is. She kept telling the detectives that she didn't know anything and didn't understand why they were questioning her. Anyway, there's a problem with Mendez's video."

"What kind of problem?"

"Mendez's security system is set up so that his camera records video in fifteen-minute loops," said Beanie, consulting the notes he'd taken during his conversation with Fields. "Meaning that every fifteen minutes, the camera records over the previous fifteen minutes. However, Mendez has the system designed to make a copy of each fifteen-minute segment to his computer so he can watch these little vignettes at a later date."

"Does Mendez have a fifteen-minute segment showing Joshua leaving the Volkov house?" asked Stevie.

"Mendez can't find a recording of Joshua leaving," said Beanie. "That's why he assumed that Joshua didn't leave the house, and I'm inclined to agree."

"What do the cops think?"

"Fields said before they conclude that Joshua went into the Volkov house, but didn't come out," said Beanie, "they want to talk to other residents on Dolphin Lane who might have surveillance cameras. Maybe another neighbor has a different angle."

"An angle that shows Joshua walking out of the Volkov house," said Stevie.

"That's what I'm hoping," said Beanie, rubbing his chin. "But, I'm worried that—"

A jaunty tune emitted from Beanie's computer.

Stevie frowned. "What's that?"

Staring at his monitor, Beanie recognized the Skype application signaling a response from him.

Surprised, Beanie said, "Someone wants to do a video call with me."

"Who?" asked Stevie.

His heart slamming, Beanie focused on the name of the caller. "It says the caller is ... Joshua ..."

Stevie gaped at him. "Joshua is calling you?"

Nodding, Beanie said, "I'm going to answer the call ..."

Minutes later, on the computer screen, a young, good-looking redhead guy stared at Beanie. And there was no mistaking who it was—Joshua Howard.

The formerly missing intern said, "Hey, Beanie ..."

"Joshua?" asked Beanie, hardly able to believe his eyes. "Where are you? Where have you been? Everybody's been looking for you."

"Dude, we thought you were dead," said Stevie.

"Well, as you can see," said Joshua. "I'm not dead … I'm alive and well."

"That you are," said Beanie, noticing Joshua's surroundings. He was sitting at a table in a small dining room. On the wall behind Joshua was a large framed poster of a woman holding a white hibiscus flower.

"Look, I just wanted to let you know that I'm fine," said Joshua. "And I'm sorry for worrying you and my family and friends."

"Who bit your finger off?" blurted Stevie.

Beanie glanced at Stevie, who had moved his chair closer to the desk, and scowled.

Stevie shrugged.

Holding up a bandaged hand, Joshua said, "I'd rather not get into that. It's kind of embarrassing. But my hand is okay. I saw a doctor, so …"

Slightly suspicious, Beanie hesitated, and then said, "Joshua, the police want to talk to you. And so do I, but not over the computer. Is there somewhere we can meet?"

Joshua's gaze cut to the left and stayed there long enough to make Beanie wonder what he was looking at. A moment later, focusing on Beanie again, Joshua cleared his throat and said, "That's not really a good idea."

"Where are you now?" asked Beanie.

"Visiting friends," said Joshua.

"He means where in the world," said Stevie.

Shaking his head, Joshua said, "Look, I am sorry that I worried you, but I just wanted you to know that I'm okay so you can let your readers know, but I have to go now."

Worried and apprehensive, Beanie said, "Joshua, wait, please. Don't—"

The screen went black, and then seconds later, flickered back to the Word document.

Beanie cursed.

"Didn't get much out of him," remarked Stevie.

"No, I didn't," said Beanie, regretting his decision to let Stevie listen in on the Skype chat. However, Beanie had a feeling the conversation wouldn't have been much different without Stevie's interference.

"But he is alive, so …"

Beanie swiveled his leather chair toward Stevie. "How did he seem to you?"

"I don't know. I mean, okay, I guess," said Stevie. "Kind of like he didn't want to talk and just wanted to get off the call as soon as possible."

Rubbing his jaw, Beanie said, "Yeah, that's what I thought, too, but …"

"But what?"

"Joshua called to tell me that he's alive and well," said Beanie. "And I'm convinced he's alive. But is he really well?"

19

"I agree with you," said Noelle as she loaded ceramic plates into the dishwasher. "Joshua is alive. But is he really well?"

As he stored the leftovers of their dinner—goat stew and pineapple rice—in plastic Tupperware bowls, Beanie said, "You know, this is going to sound crazy, but …"

"But …?" asked Noelle, adding detergent to the dishwasher.

"But after I talked to Joshua, I kept replaying the conversation in my mind, and I started to get the strangest feeling," said Beanie. "A weird, paranoid feeling like, what if someone is holding Joshua hostage? Someone who forced him to do a video chat with me to prove that he's okay, you know. I know it seems farfetched."

"But what if it's not?" asked Noelle.

Beanie said, "I keep thinking of those movies where they show a close up of a person on the phone, telling someone they're okay, and then they cut to a wide shot, and there's someone standing behind them with a gun."

"From what you told me," said Noelle. "Joshua was sitting at a table, probably facing a laptop."

Still reeling from the conversation with Joshua, Beanie said, "I could see quite a bit of his background. The only thing behind him was a huge poster. A woman holding a white hibiscus, I think."

"White hibiscus?" questioned Noelle. "Reminds me of Rufus Mason. Remember I saw him buying a white hibiscus at the nursery."

Beanie frowned. "Interesting …"

Noelle closed the dishwasher then pressed several buttons to start the machine. "Maybe the person with the gun was standing at the other end of the table, out of view. Or, maybe to the side of Joshua, but still out of view."

Rubbing his jaw, Beanie said, "Maybe. I just wish Joshua would have told me where he was. I wish he would have agreed to meet with me and the fact that he rushed off the Skype call makes me think …"

"You think something is wrong," said Noelle.

Beanie sighed. "And I feel like I'm the only one."

"What do you mean?"

"When I talked to Vivian about it," said Beanie, "She requested a follow-up story to let our readers know that Joshua is okay, but when I told her I wasn't quite sure about that, she didn't share my suspicions."

"Maybe that's because she wasn't there when he called," suggested Noelle.

"Well, Stevie was with me when Joshua called, and he thinks I'm reading too much into things," said Beanie.

"You have to trust your instincts, Roland," said Noelle. "If you think something is not right with Joshua, then you need to keep investigating."

"I keep thinking about Mendez's video," said Beanie.

Leaning against the kitchen counter, Noelle asked, "Did the cops find any other video footage showing a different angle?"

"Not yet," said Beanie. "But I don't think they're going to find any footage that shows Joshua leaving the Volkov house because there is no footage showing that. Because Joshua didn't leave that house."

Tilting her head, Noelle asked, "You think Natalya Volkov is holding Joshua hostage?"

"I know it seems crazy," said Beanie. "And I have no proof, but maybe it's not so crazy, after all. Joshua went to the Volkovs to tell them he would expose the secret about Natalya unless they paid him. I'm sure there was an argument. Natalya attacked Joshua and bit his finger off. Joshua might have passed out and …"

"And then the Volkovs locked Joshua in a bedroom or something?" asked Noelle.

Pinching the bridge of his nose, Beanie said, "I know it's ridiculous. Makes no sense. Why would Natalya hold Joshua hostage?"

"Why would she kill her husband?" asked Noelle. "We both know she did it, and even the cops think so. Why would she attack all those people in the Aerie Islands? The woman is psychotic. Meaning, there's no rational reason for her homicidal tendencies. Meaning, maybe she is holding Joshua against his will. And if that's true, Roland, then you have to find out … "

"An arrest was made this morning in the murder of Ivan Volkov," said Officer Damon Fields.

Beanie pressed the 'Speaker' button on his phone, then turned to his computer and opened a Word file to type notes. "Who was arrested?"

"Natalya Volkov," said Fields.

Shocked, and yet relieved as a sense of vindication washed over him, Beanie asked, "Did her prints come back as a match for the prints you found on the murder weapon?"

"There's no physical evidence linking her to the murder," said Fields. "Mrs. Volkov confessed to killing her husband."

"Natalya confessed?" Beanie shook his head, even though Fields couldn't see him. "When?"

"A few days ago," said Fields, "after your story came out about Joshua Howard and how he was never missing, your neighbor Mendez came down to the station with more found footage from his video surveillance files."

"Did he find the video of Joshua leaving the Volkov house?" asked Beanie, hopeful, but cautious. He'd spent the last few days trying to think of how to find out if Natalya was, in fact, holding Joshua hostage. Other than breaking into the Volkov house and searching every room, he hadn't come up with an effective investigative strategy. Knocking on the Volkov's front door and talking to Natalya was pointless. Beanie had tried, and each time, his knocks and doorbell rings had gone unanswered.

Fields said, "It's a video of Natalya Volkov attacking Ivan in their driveway."

"Are you serious?"

"The timestamp on the video is the day before Ivan was found dead in the jungle. Natalya and Ivan get out of their car a little after midnight," said Fields. "You can tell they're arguing. Gesturing wildly. Ivan grabs her arm and drags her into the house. A few minutes later, Ivan exits the house and walks toward the car. Then Natalya comes out, and she is holding a knife."

Beanie was floored. "A knife?"

"Natalya runs up to Ivan, brandishing the knife at him," said Fields. "She doesn't stab him, but they continue to argue, and then they get back into the car and drive off."

Furiously typing notes, Beanie asked, "Any idea where they went?"

"We're still trying to determine that," said Fields. "What we do know is that when the Volkov's car returned two hours later, only Natalya got out of the car."

"Where was Ivan?" asked Beanie, fingers flying over the keyboard.

"That's what the detectives wanted to ask Natalya," said Fields. "So they went to talk with her. They confronted her about Mendez's video. She starts ranting and raving about Mendez being wrong."

"What did she mean by that?" asked Beanie.

"I don't know," said Fields. "But Natalya became very agitated, and she lunged at one of the detectives. Growled at him and scratched his face pretty bad. So they brought her down to the station. When she arrived, they booked her for assaulting a police officer, and they had a devil of a time trying to control her. She fought all the way to the jail cell."

"Not surprised," Beanie said, a foreboding chill washing over him as he recalled the widow's transformation from a timid mourner to a deranged person when he'd tried to interview her.

Fields said, "She was fit to be tied. We had a time trying to calm her down. She kept shouting that she would never hurt Ivan, and she didn't kill him. Once we finally got her in the cell, one of the detectives went to talk to her again, and she told him a slightly different story."

"Different how?"

"Natalya Volkov said she couldn't remember if she'd killed her husband, or not, but she didn't think she had," said Fields. "But then she said that if she had killed him, it was not her but the wolf within her that possesses her. So they asked her to submit to a polygraph test."

Beanie said, "I'm guessing she failed."

"She did," confirmed Fields. "Then she started carrying on again, saying the wolf within her must have killed Ivan. She claimed she hadn't meant to kill her husband, but the wolf took over. So, she was arrested."

Beanie asked, "Are the detective sure the charges will stick without any physical evidence to connect Natalya to the murder? Natalya's actions on Mendez's surveillance video is suspicious, but it doesn't show her stabbing Ivan."

"Well, that is a problem with the case," said Fields. "But we're hoping that the saliva and the prints on the murder weapon will come back as a match for Natalya Volkov."

After ending the call with Fields, Beanie met with Stevie and Vivian to update them. Vivian agreed with Stevie's suggestion for the headline – *ARREST IN JUNGLE CORPSE MURDER*. Side by side with Stevie, Beanie found the collaboration quick and easy. They wrote the story in about two hours. After editing and a few revisions, the article was featured on the *Palmchat Gazette* website by five o'clock that evening. Like the other jungle corpse murder stories, the piece went viral, trending in both the Palmchat Islands and throughout the Aerie Islands.

Around six p.m., when Beanie decided to call it a day, Stevie ambled into Beanie's cubicle and announced, "Natalya Volkov was bailed out of jail an hour ago. Dr. Zeller paid the bond."

"Dr. Zeller?" Beanie gaped at Stevie.

Nodding, Stevie said, "Turns out he's more than just her landlord."

"Meaning?"

"Zeller was her therapist," said Stevie. "He treated her when she was a teenager."

"How do you know that?"

Stevie explained that he'd done some digging and come across Zeller's name in a deposition related to one of the lawsuits against the Volkovs. In the deposition, Zeller explained his relationship to Natalya.

Returning to his desk, Beanie sat down, fired up his computer, and asked, "Why was Zeller treating Natalya? Is she bipolar or something?"

"Apparently, according to his deposition, Dr. Zeller worked with children and teenagers diagnosed with dissociative identity disorder—commonly known as DID. He treated patients diagnosed with a rare form of the condition. They didn't have split personalities. Instead, these patients believed they turned into animals."

"You're kidding?" said Beanie, opening a Word file to take notes.

Shaking his head, Stevie said, "Zeller explained to the lawyers that the patient, when presented with extreme trauma they can't deal with, creates an animal persona, for lack of a better word. In those moments, the person doesn't see themselves as a person, but as—"

"A wolf," said Beanie. "That's what happened to Natalya Volkov when she lunged at me. She was snarling and growling. She thought she was a wolf. The stress and trauma of my questions about her husband's death were too much for her to bear, so she split into the animal persona."

"Makes sense," said Stevie. "As Natalya Volkov, she probably feels inadequate and helpless, maybe hopeless, but as a wolf, she's powerful and strong."

"And she attacks," said Beanie, stroking his chin. "And she bites, which also makes sense. If she believes she's a wolf, then she does what wolves do. She kept saying she had a sickness in her blood. She must have meant the DID. Did Zeller say anything about how to help someone like her?"

Stevie said, "Zeller proposed several treatments, one of which was shock therapy combined with anti-psychotic meds. Who knows if Natalya took the treatments, or if she did, whether they worked?"

"Considering that Natalya attacked countless people and eventually killed her husband, probably while under the influence of her animal persona, I doubt Zeller's therapy worked," said Beanie. "I'd like to talk to him about Natalya. Get a quote from the doctor who tried, and failed, to cure her homicidal tendencies."

21

The following day, around two in the afternoon, Beanie sat in the office of Dr. Walter Zeller. He nursed a cup of coffee the child psychologist offered him when Beanie knocked on the doctor's front door, requesting an interview.

Beanie had prepared himself for Zeller's refusal to speak with him, but the psychologist didn't put up a fight. He wasn't very welcoming, either, but at least there was no hostility in his tone or demeanor. Zeller agreed to answer a few questions, but Beanie got the feeling that the doctor would politely ask him to leave if the interrogation got too intense.

"I'll cut to the chase," said Beanie.

"That would be wise," advised Zeller.

Beanie cleared his throat. "I want to talk about your relationship with Natalya Volkov."

"What do you want to know about it?"

Regarding the doctor, who seemed guarded and suspicious despite the pleasant smile on his face, Beanie wondered how to approach the man. Should he ask Zeller questions he already knew the answers to, in an effort to see if Zeller would be truthful? Or, should he be honest? Beanie hadn't decided whether to play his cards close to the vest or lay his cards on the table.

"As I'm sure you know, I'm covering Ivan Volkov's murder for the *Palmchat Gazette*," said Beanie.

"I am aware," said Zeller, eyes narrowing slightly as he made a steeple of his fingers.

Beanie squirmed in his seat, suspecting that the man was examining him, analyzing him, coming to conclusions about Beanie's mental state. "Right, so ... we learned a few days ago that you bailed Natalya Volkov out of jail."

SUSPECT IN JUNGLE CORPSE MURDER RELEASED, written by Stevie, had been short and sweet, identifying Zeller as the person who'd made Natalya Volkov's temporary freedom possible.

Dr. Zeller said, "That was in your article, was it not?"

Beanie nodded, still feeling as though he was under the microscope. "What we didn't have was your comment."

"I have no comment about that."

Not surprised that Dr. Zeller was stonewalling him, Beanie said, "You must have some reason why you paid her bail."

"My reasons are no one's business," said Zeller, head tilted to the left. "I don't care to divulge them."

"Was it because you've known Natalya for so long?" questioned Beanie, adopting a more aggressive stance. "Since she was fourteen, right? That's when you started treating her for dissociative identity disorder."

The psychologist scowled and leaned forward. "How did you find out about that? Patient records are protected by—"

"Relax, okay," said Beanie. "No patient records were breached or stolen. We read the deposition you took when Natalya was sued. You explained the relationship to the plaintiff's attorney and tried to make him understand Natalya's condition."

Exhaling, Zeller pinched the bridge of his nose. "You don't understand. I had no choice."

"What do you mean?"

"Natalya is all alone in the world. Now that Ivan is dead, she has no one ..."

"No one except you."

"She has always had me," said Dr. Zeller. "And she always will ..."

Not quite sure what to make of that declaration, if anything, Beanie cleared his throat and asked, "Since you bailed Natalya out of jail, I'm assuming you don't think she killed her husband."

"Her arrest was a grave travesty, a miscarriage of justice," ranted Zeller. "She was treated quite unfairly, and for what? Because of some misguide stereotypical belief that the spouse must have done it?"

"Natalya was seen on a neighbor's surveillance video threatening Ivan with a knife," said Beanie. "The day before Ivan's murder, she and Ivan left their home in the middle of the night, but only Natalya returned."

Waving a dismissive hand, Dr. Zeller said, "They argued. Natalya didn't mean to brandish the knife. Ivan decided to spend the night at a nearby motel to give Natalya some space. Mendez is a nosey old fool who harbors spite and malice towards Natalya. I can't believe the police gave credence to his so-called evidence. The man should not have been taken seriously, considering that his video proves nothing and was taken out of context."

Beanie said, "What about the fact that Natalya confessed to the murder of her husband? Were her words also taken out of context?"

Zeller's eyes narrowed, giving him a shrewd, disgusting appearance. "I am sure Natalya's lawyer will be able to get that confession thrown out and prove it was a false confession given under extreme duress."

"Who did Natalya hire to represent her?"

"I retained the attorney for Natalya," said Dr. Zeller. "Octavia Constant. She is the best defense attorney in the Palmchat Islands."

"Yes, I know," said Beanie, remembering how Octavia Constant had helped Noelle when his wife was accused of a heinous crime she didn't commit. "But, Dr. Zeller, the police are confident that Natalya killed Ivan. And with her history of attacking people—"

"Natalya has a terrible disease of the mind," said Dr. Zeller. "I have tried for years to help Natalya with her psychosis."

"A psychosis that causes her to attack and bite people," said Beanie.

Dr. Zeller said, "She has a severe advanced case of lycanthropy. Natalya believes she is a wolf. She bites people to fulfill a delusional fantasy to prove that she is a wolf."

"Are you currently treating her?" asked Beanie.

Nodding, Dr. Zeller said, "I am retired. However, I consented to continue treating Natalya. I wanted her to be institutionalized, but Ivan refused. I was able to convince him to move to Oyster Farms so I could treat her and observe her progress."

"You actually thought it was a good idea for a woman who thinks she's a wolf to move to a neighborhood where there are lots of young children?" asked Beanie, indignation rising within him.

Dr. Zeller's face reddened as he looked away for a moment. "In hindsight, it was probably not the best idea, but I was convinced that I could help Natalya overcome her struggles."

"But, you weren't able to, were you?" asked Beanie, unable to mask the censure in his tone.

The psychologist sighed. "I was unable to find a way to help Natalya control her dark impulses."

"Dark impulses?" Beanie shook his head. "Is that why you told me not to take my boys to the Volkov house on Halloween? Were you afraid Natalya might not be able to control her dark impulses?"

Dr. Zeller said, "There's no need to worry anymore. The neighborhood is safe from her now."

"What does that mean?"

"With the help of Attorney Constant," said Dr. Zeller, "Natalya was admitted to the Rakestraw-Blake Center. She is in police custody at the facility until her trial."

Somewhat relieved, Beanie said, "Well, that's good to know."

"I figured you would think so," said Dr. Zeller. "Now, if there's nothing else—"

"I have one last question," said Beanie. "Did Natalya have anything to do with Joshua Howard's disappearance?"

"Joshua Howard? You mean the impertinent young man who tried to extort Natalya and Ivan?" asked Zeller, lips curled in a cruel sneer.

A spark of defense rose in Beanie. "I mean my intern, who sued the Volkovs and then disappeared—"

"But, he wasn't really missing," said Zeller. "At least, that's what I read in your article. So how could Natalya have had anything to do with his so-called disappearance? He probably left town after his blackmail attempts failed."

"Joshua wasn't trying to extort the Volkovs," said Beanie. "He was seeking compensation for injuries that Natalya caused when she lunged at him and bit his shoulder."

"Natalya was not in her right mind when she did that," said Zeller, "which Ivan acknowledged. He offered to pay Joshua's medical bills, but the greedy little ingrate wanted more, so he filed a frivolous lawsuit."

"How was it frivolous when Natalya attacked him?"

Again, Zeller waved his hand dismissively. "Yes, she bit him, but the wound was not as severe as he and his attorney alleged. Her teeth broke the skin, yes, but they did not shatter bone. Joshua Howard wasn't maimed or rendered unable to work. He embellished his injuries, most likely at the urging of his greedy lawyer."

Beanie took a quick breath, trying to quell his frustration. Zeller's opinion of Joshua's lawyer brought to mind the Taylors' judgments about the attorney, which Friday had corroborated. Beanie hated to think Joshua had been led astray by a lawyer who'd convinced him to exaggerate his injuries.

"Now, as I said before if there's nothing else—"

Standing, Beanie said, "No, there isn't."

22

"I've already found the better suspect," announced Attorney Octavia Constant when Beanie reached her several days later for a comment.

"Can I quote you on that?" asked Beanie, typing notes into the Word filed he'd opened.

"You absolutely can," consented Octavia.

"What about Natalya's confession that she killed her husband?" asked Beanie.

"That was a false confession," said Octavia.

"You think she was forced to confess to murder?" asked Beanie, aware that the confession would be inadmissible if Octavia could prove that the St. Killian detective had coerced Natalya into incriminating herself.

"I think it was an internalized confession," said Octavia. "That's a type of false confession where the confessor actually believes they committed the crime. Those sorts of confessions can occur if the person has a mental disorder. They can also result from very aggressive interrogation techniques."

"What about the polygraph test she failed?" asked Beanie.

Octavia said, "Lie detector tests have been proven unreliable time and again in courts all over the world. And Natalya Volkov should never have been given that test considering her dissociative identity disorder. There's no way the test provided accurate or objective results."

"So who is the better suspect?" asked Beanie.

"I would tell you," said Octavia, "but I don't want that in the *Palmchat Gazette*, for obvious reasons."

"Would you tell me if I promised not to publish that detail?" asked Beanie.

Octavia said, "I've always been able to trust you to keep your word, so …
"

"So…?" prompted Beanie, anxious for the information.

"I actually have two better suspects," said Octavia.

"Two suspects?"

"The first better suspect is someone you know pretty well."

Confused, Beanie asked, "Who?"

"Joshua Howard," said Octavia. "Your missing intern who wasn't missing."

"Are you serious?" asked Beanie scoffing. "You think Joshua killed Ivan? How did you come up with that?"

"I'm sure you've heard about Anthony Mendez's surveillance video," said Octavia, "which seems to show Natalya and Ivan arguing—"

"It also shows Natalya wielding a knife at Ivan," pointed out Beanie.

"But it doesn't explain why the Volkovs were arguing," said Octavia. "It doesn't explain why Natalya had the knife."

"I think it's obvious why she had the knife," said Beanie.

"That night when they argued," said Octavia, "it was because Ivan wanted to meet with Joshua, but Natalya didn't want him to do that."

"They were arguing about Joshua?" asked Beanie, skeptical.

"Ivan had received a call from Joshua, who wanted to meet to discuss the lawsuit," said Octavia. "Ivan wanted to go, to settle their conflict with Joshua once and for all. Natalya begged Ivan not to go. She was worried about him. She didn't want him to go alone, but Ivan didn't want her to go with him, so he took her into the house. Then Ivan walked out to the car. Natalya followed him. She had the knife because she was desperate to stop Ivan from leaving without her. Ivan relented, and the two of them went to meet with Joshua."

"Where did they go to meet him?" asked Beanie.

"A motel in Little Turkey," said Octavia. "Ivan convinced Natalya to let him meet with Joshua alone, and then he told her to drive home and wait for him to call her once the meeting with Joshua was over. That's why Natalya returned to the house alone."

"And what happened during the meeting with Ivan and Joshua?" asked Beanie.

"Natalya doesn't know," said Octavia. "What she knows is that Ivan never called her to pick him up from the motel in Little Turkey. And then, the next afternoon, the police were knocking at her door, telling her that her husband had been found dead. Stabbed to death in the jungle."

"Which I'm sure she already knew," countered Beanie. "Considering that she probably drove him to the jungle, stabbed him, and—"

"Look, I know you don't want to think that your intern is a cold-blooded killer, but—"

"Joshua didn't kill Ivan," said Beanie, dismissing Octavia's unfounded theories. "Who's your other suspect?"

"Rufus Mason."

"Mason?" Beanie was shocked. "What makes you think he killed Ivan Volkov?"

"Natalya said Rufus Mason threatened to kill her husband," said Octavia.

"Are you serious?"

"That's what she said," said Octavia. "She told me one of her neighbors wanted Ivan dead. When I asked her to tell me the neighbor's name, Natalya wasn't able to remember, but she said he was the neighbor who killed his wife. Rufus Mason killed his wife."

"That's just a rumor," said Beanie.

Octavia exhaled. "Roland, you and I both know if that tree in Mason's backyard is ever dug up, we'll find his wife's remains."

"It's never been proven that Mason's wife is dead."

"Roland—"

"I talked to Natalya," said Beanie. "She didn't mention anything about Rufus Mason wanting to kill her husband. She had no idea who might have wanted to kill him."

"When you spoke to her," said Octavia, "she hadn't taken her meds."

"Is that why she attacked me?" asked Beanie.

"Most likely. According to Dr. Zeller, Ivan always made sure that Natalya took her pills," said Octavia. "After he was killed, Natalya stopped taking them. At the Rakestraw-Blake Center, she's been on a strict protocol of medication, which helps her think more clearly and rationally. This medication also helps her recall memories."

Skeptical, Beanie asked, "And she recalled Rufus Mason threatening to kill her husband?"

"Is that a hint of dubiousness I hear in your tone?"

"It's more than a hint," admitted Beanie. "Natalya's claim seems to be coming from out of the blue."

"Actually, it makes sense," said Octavia. "Considering the reason why Ivan Volkov was killed."

23

"I still can't believe Rufus Mason would kill Ivan Volkov," said Noelle, shaking her head as she put a K-cup in the Keurig machine.

"Me neither," said Beanie, rubbing his eyes, trying to wake up. "But Mason is the only neighbor rumored to have killed his wife."

Normally, at six in the morning, he was bright-eyed, if not always bushy-tailed, and eager for a pre-dawn cup of java with his wife. But last night had been exhausting. Not only had the boys been rambunctious and recalcitrant, but following their baths and bedtime stories, Beanie hadn't been able to sleep. The conversation with Octavia Constant yesterday weighed heavily on his mind. He'd shared the defense attorney's shocking revelations with Noelle, and they'd stayed up for several hours discussing the details.

"Don't you think it's weird that Natalya Volkov would accuse Mason?" asked Noelle, placing a steaming mug of black coffee in front of Beanie. "I didn't think there was any bad blood between them. I thought the Volkovs had gotten into it with Old Wilson."

Beanie took a sip of the hot coffee and looked at the ceiling. "According to Octavia, Mason didn't kill Ivan Volkov over any bad blood."

"Then why did Mason kill Ivan?"

Glancing at his wife, Beanie said, "Octavia said Natalya claims that Rufus Mason is a Fury follower."

"A Fury follower?" asked Noelle.

As his wife joined him at the table with her mug of coffee, Beanie nodded. "Apparently, Mason killed Ivan in honor of the Fury."

"In honor of the Fury?" Noelle shook her head. "I don't understand."

"I wish I didn't," said Beanie, struggling to shrug off the apprehension that had plagued him since his conversation with Octavia.

"What do you mean?"

"You know the Fury has people who are obsessed and fascinated with him," said Beanie, taking another sip.

"I've heard of Fury followers," said Noelle. "They revere him and don't seem to mind that he's a sick, twisted serial killer. They don't care that he terrorized the islands. That he mutilated people, often when they were still alive."

"Well, this isn't public knowledge," confided Beanie. "And I only know because Octavia told me, but apparently, you can't just decide to follow the Fury. If you want to follow him, you have to kill for him."

Noelle gasped. "Are you serious?"

"I wish I weren't," said Beanie.

"I wish I could say that it horrifies me, but …"

Surprised, Beanie asked, "It doesn't horrify you?"

"It does, and yet it doesn't," said Noelle. "I don't know how to explain it, but … this whole idea about having to kill someone to follow the Fury reminds me of a street-level gang initiation."

Beanie reached across the table and placed his hand on Noelle's arm.

"Before my father could join Vadaj," said Noelle, "he had to kill a guy to prove that he could become an assassin."

As his wife brought the coffee mug to her lips, Beanie tried not to stiffen, but he felt his body go rigid at the mention of Vadaj. As the execution arm of the PC-5, the Vadaj family had created a deadly faction of brutal, cold-hearted killers responsible for protecting the cartel through intimidation, threats, and murder.

Noelle's father, Josue Chartres, had been one of the gang's deadliest enforcers, eventually fulfilling the Death List, a dreaded document for the doomed, those who dared to try to bring down the cartel.

"Anyway, I have doubts about Natalya's story," said Beanie, pivoting back to the original topic. Discussing Noelle's father always bothered him. He wasn't sure how to feel about his notorious father-in-law, a man he'd never met. Her dad repulsed him, and yet stories about the man always conjured up a lurid fascination. Beanie wanted to know more, but didn't know if he could stomach it, didn't know if he could remain impartial. Noelle wasn't close to her father, but Beanie knew his harsh judgment would offend her.

"I don't believe her, either," said Noelle, sitting her mug on the table.

"I mean, I doubt that Rufus Mason wanted to be a Fury follower," said Beanie. "If you have to kill to become a Fury follower, then Rufus Mason should already be a follower."

Noelle asked, "You mean because he killed his wife?"

"Allegedly," amended Beanie. "But, let's say it's true. That means Mason fulfilled the requirements to become a Fury follower."

"Unless Mason didn't kill his wife," said Noelle. "There's no proof of that."

Sighing, Beanie glanced at the remaining coffee in his mug. "That's what I told Octavia. Nobody knows if Mason's wife is dead. Maybe she ran off and left Mason."

"But, if Mason didn't kill his wife," said Noelle, "then he didn't meet the Fury follower requirements, so that means he needed to kill someone—Ivan Volkov."

"Why choose Ivan Volkov?" wondered Beanie. "Mason was accused of killing his wife more than twenty years ago. Why would Mason wait so long to find another potential victim?"

"That is strange," said Noelle. "Tell me this—how does Natalya Volkov know that Rufus Mason wants to follow the Fury?"

"Octavia said Natalya told her that Ivan found out somehow," said Beanie. "Of course, Natalya didn't know or couldn't remember how Ivan found out."

"What about Octavia's other better suspect?" asked Noelle.

Beanie glanced at his wife. "Are you serious? Joshua is not a better suspect."

"Are you sure?" asked Noelle.

"What?" Beanie shook his head. "Elle, how can you possibly believe that Joshua killed Ivan?"

"Octavia said that Natalya and Ivan were arguing about Joshua before they left to meet with Joshua at that motel in Little Turkey," said Noelle. "But Ivan never returned to the house."

"Octavia repeated some cockamamie story that Natalya came up with," said Beanie. "But, how can anything Natalya claims be trusted? Babe, this is a woman who thinks she's a wolf. She attacks people. She lunges and bites. I told you how she lunged at the cops."

"I know that," said Noelle, nodding. "And it's not that I think Joshua is a killer, but you always say that journalism has to be objective, looked at from all angles, and you can't jump to conclusions, or—"

"I'm not jumping to conclusions about Natalya," said Beanie. "She killed her husband. And I know there's not much evidence to prove that, but I know it's true. She's a dangerous psychopath, and I'm glad she's no longer living down the street from us."

24

"You have a visitor waiting in the conference room," announced Millie as Beanie strolled through the spacious, airy lobby of the *Palmchat Gazette* office.

An hour or so ago, he and Stevie had left the building and walked the three blocks to Pourciau Square. They'd gotten take-out from the Nanny Goat, one of Beanie's favorite food trucks, found a table in the palm tree-dotted park area, and discussed the direction of their follow-up to JUNGLE CORPSE ATTORNEY FINDS BETTER SUSPECT. The article, which detailed Natalya's mental illness and past issues in the Aerie Islands, provided details about Beanie's conversation with the defense attorney.

Like most of the other articles related to the Volkov murder, the most recent story, written four days ago, had been wildly popular. The island's residents couldn't get enough of the "jungle corpse murder," as Ivan Volkov's death was now being referred to, and Vivian wanted them to give the public what they wanted. After all, the more clicks a story got, the more the *Palmchat Gazette* could charge for advertising.

What the story didn't mention, per his agreement with Octavia, was the identity of her "better suspects," one of whom was Joshua Howard.

Beanie still couldn't believe that Octavia had seriously contemplated the idea of Joshua as Ivan Volkov's killer. If anything, Volkov had a much better motive to kill Joshua, considering he'd thought the intern was trying to blackmail him. Admittedly, Natalya's claim that Ivan had met Joshua at a motel in Little Turkey the day before Ivan was found dead was concerning. But was it true? Beanie wanted to hear Joshua's side of the story, but since the Skype video call weeks ago, Beanie hadn't been able to reach the intern. Once again, Joshua had gone off the grid and had ignored Beanie's repeated attempts to contact him.

Stevie, walking behind Beanie, asked, "Who me?"

Millie shook her head. "No, Roland."

"A visitor?" asked Beanie, trying to remember if he'd scheduled a meeting with a witness, or a confidential source.

"A rather interesting young lady," said Millie, raising an arched eyebrow. "I told her you were at lunch, and I wasn't sure when you would return, but she insisted on staying because, according to her, it is a matter of extreme importance."

"This rather interesting young lady have a name?" asked Beanie.

"Friday H. Smith," said Millie. "She claimed the two of you have spoken before about Joshua Howard."

Nodding, Beanie said, "We have."

"Wonder what the matter of extreme importance is?" asked Stevie.

"That's what I'm going to find out," said Beanie. After thanking Millie for relaying the message, he headed to the conference room.

Inside the large space normally used for staff meetings, Beanie found Friday pacing around the large, oblong mahogany table, alternately pulling her bottom lip and throwing her head back, as though studying the ceiling tiles for some sign.

Clearing his throat to announce his presence, Beanie entered cautiously, wary of the melodramatic young woman, worried her theatrics might give him indigestion.

Pirouetting to face Beanie, Friday said, "I need some advice."

Beanie stared at Joshua Howard's girlfriend, dressed in her typically bright and colorful attire – a pink skirt, neon green blouse, and red heels.

"What kind of advice do you need?" asked Beanie, taking a seat at the table.

Following a heaving, theatrical sigh, she said, "Actually, on second thought, it's not really advice I need, because I know what I have to do, but I don't know how to do it. So, you know what? Maybe I do need advice."

Struggling to temper his frustration, Beanie asked, "With what?"

"I need to talk to Octavia Constant."

Beanie stared at the woman's swooping pompadour. "Why?"

"I read the story you wrote about her," said Friday as she walked to the wall of ceiling-to-floor glass windows. "The article said she found a better suspect for the murder of Ivan Volkov. Did she tell you who it was?"

"She did," said Beanie. "But she told me in confidence, and I can't tell you—"

"I don't need you to tell me," said Friday, her back to him. "But, you need to tell Octavia that she's wrong."

Beanie was doubtful of her claim. "Wrong about the better suspect?"

Nodding, Friday said, "It's not who she thinks it is …"

Beanie wondered how Friday knew who Octavia had identified as the better suspect, but instead, he asked, "Then … who is it?"

She faced Beanie, her eyes brimming with tears. "The better suspect is … Joshua."

25

Shocked and suspicious, Beanie stared at Friday H. Smith. "Joshua? Are you sure?"

"I wish I wasn't," said Friday, shaking her head. "But the evidence against him is too compelling!"

"What evidence?"

"This evidence." Friday rushed back to the table, dropped down into a chair, and then picked up a backpack she must have placed in the empty chair next to her. "You know Joshua dumped me, right?"

Beanie shook his head. "No, I didn't—"

"Yeah, well, he did," said Friday. "The day after he Skyped you, he texted me. *Texted*. Can you believe that? He couldn't tell me in person. Couldn't even bother to call me so I could hear his voice when he told me that it was over between us."

Beanie said, "Well, maybe he—"

"Anyway, after Joshua dumped me, I packed up some of his crap that he left at my apartment. Most of it was a bunch of clothes, but I found these things in an old duffle bag that belonged to him."

Beanie stared at Friday as she pulled a laptop and a 9 x 12 manila envelope from the backpack and placed them on the table.

"I opened the envelope and checked the contents," said Friday. "Very disturbing stuff."

"What about the laptop?"

"I don't know the password," she said. "I tried to figure it out, but I couldn't."

"I might be able to help with that," said Beanie, thinking of Stevie's hacker cousin.

"You should take a look at this stuff," said Friday, pushing the envelope toward him. "And then maybe you can give it to Octavia Constant. Or, maybe the police should have it. I don't know. All I know is … just take a look yourself."

Wary, Beanie removed the contents from the manila envelope.

A small spiral-bound notebook.

And a letter folded into thirds.

"Read the notebook first," advised Friday. "It'll help you understand the letter."

"This belongs to Joshua?" asked Beanie, picking up the notebook. Opening it, he stared at the large, child-like block print.

"It's his," confirmed Friday. "I recognize his handwriting."

Beanie opened the spiral notebook and read the first page.

Target: Volkov
Objective: take him down
9/23 – Volkov leaves home/goes to work/Vaughn Pharma/lunch w/coworkers/home
9/24 – same old same old
9/27 – same old same old

"Target Volkov?" Beanie stared across the table at Friday. "So I'm guessing this is about Joshua's lawyer telling him to get leverage on the Volkovs?"

Shaking her head, Friday asked, "That's what I thought at first, but I was wrong."

"How were you wrong?" asked Beanie, studying the notations next to the dates. "You told me that Joshua started following Volkov to get dirt on him. Seems like that's what he was doing. He observed Volkov leaving his house, going to work."

"Joshua wasn't looking for dirt. He was looking for an opportunity to get rid of Volkov," said Friday. "That's why he was following him. He had to get Volkov's schedule down, so he could determine the best time to go after him."

"Maybe," remarked Beanie, though he wasn't sure. He wasn't ready to affirm Friday's conclusions. He turned past several blank pages, stopped at the next entry, and read:

Target: Volkov
Objective: attack when least expected
9/30 – argument with neighbor

Beanie asked, "What's the argument with the neighbor? Was Joshua talking about an argument he'd had with one of his neighbors?"

Friday said, "That's my guess."

"But why is that entry under the heading Objective: attack when least expected?" Beanie wondered out loud.

"I don't know," said Friday. "That entry is weird. I don't think it has anything to do with Volkov."

"It must, though, don't you think?" asked Beanie. "Or why would he write it in the notebook? Maybe Volkov argued with a neighbor?"

Friday said, "I guess that's possible. The notebook is proof that Joshua was stalking Volkov. Watching him. He could have seen Volkov arguing with a neighbor."

Rubbing his jaw, Beanie considered Friday's speculation. What neighbor could Volkov have been arguing with? Old Wilson came to mind, but Beanie dismissed him. The old coot had beef with the Volkovs, but it had started after Old Wilson claimed that Natalya bit him more than a month later. Beanie didn't recall any previous altercations between the old man and the young Russian couple.

Beanie turned to the next entry:

Target: Volkov
Objective: put him in the dirt
Oct. 3 – picked up package from 3110 Dolphin Lane/headed to
Tiverton
Oct. 17 – for 6 months have sent package to Tiverton
Oct. 24 – confrontation and lies

"3110 Dolphin Lane," said Beanie, familiar the address. "That's—"

"The Volkov's house," said Friday. "Joshua picks up a package, and then he goes to Tiverton. That one makes no sense to me. Joshua doesn't know anyone who's in prison."

Beanie studied the entry. "Maybe he meant the package was heading to Tiverton. The package he picked up from the Volkov's house on October third was going to be delivered to Tiverton."

"So, the Volkovs sent a package to someone at Tiverton?"

Nodding, Beanie said, "That's what I'm thinking. And looks like they might have been sending packages to Tiverton for six months. Guess Joshua found that out."

"Probably would have been easy to do," said Friday. "He could have searched the delivery company's records."

"What is confrontation and lies about?" asked Beanie. "Did he confront someone, and they lied?"

"I don't know," admitted Friday. "Maybe."

"And if so, who did he confront?" asked Beanie as he flipped past more blank pages, looking for the next entry. "Ivan Volkov?"

"That would make sense," agreed Friday. "Or, maybe Joshua was confronted by Ivan Volkov? Maybe Volkov caught Joshua following him, confronted him, and Joshua lied about stalking him."

Beanie found the next entry and read:

Target: new focus
Objective: secrets will be uncovered
Oct. 25 – introductions and confessions/told him we have
something in common—the Fury
Oct. 25 – admitted obsession with Fury
Oct. 26 – said Volkov must die

Looking up, he stared at Friday. "What the ..."

Exhaling, she said, "Guess you got to the entry about the Fury and how Volkov has to die."

Beanie struggled to manage his shock as he reread the entries, forcing himself to make sense of the disturbing words.

"Okay, so Joshua met someone," said Beanie. "And they have something in common."

"The Fury," whispered Friday. "Joshua was obsessed with him. Says so right there in his notebook."

Trying to ignore the apprehension slicing through him, Beanie asked, "Did you know that Joshua was obsessed with the Fury?"

Eyes widened, Friday asked, "Do you think I would have anything to do with him if I knew that? I don't even know how to process this. I was in love with a guy who had a thing for a twisted, disgusting serial killer. What does that say about me?"

"Obviously, you didn't know," said Beanie, irritated by Friday's melodrama, which hampered his ability to speculate.

"But don't you think I should have known?" she asked. "Don't you think—"

"There are no more entries after this one," said Beanie, flipping quickly through the pages, which were all blank, until he came to the end of the spiral notebook.

"Now, you have to read the letter," said Friday. "But I have to warn you ... it's very ... I don't even know the right word to describe it."

Annoyed by her ominous tone, Beanie picked up the letter and unfolded it. Hesitating, he skimmed the double-spaced print, recognizing the Times New Roman serif font. Apprehension took another swipe through him, and he immediately chided himself. He was being ridiculous, allowing Friday's fear to influence him. What was there to be afraid of?

Beanie read the letter.

Moments later, he wished he hadn't.

"Now do you understand?" asked Friday, her tone beseeching, her gaze imploring. "The evidence is clear. Joshua is a Fury Follower, and he killed Ivan Volkov."

26

At his desk in his small cubicle, Beanie rubbed his eyes and tried to think. Two days had passed since his meeting with Friday, when she'd pushed the 9 x 12 envelope across the table, and he'd removed the items.

Things he couldn't believe were real.

Recalling the contents still sent a shiver through him.

The small 3-by-5 spiral-bound notebook had been horrific, leaving him disillusioned and devastated.

But the type-written letter he'd read had felt like a kick in the guts.

Disturbed, Beanie thought about the signature. *Forever, your faithful follower.*

Together with Stevie and Vivian, Beanie had spent the past two days examining, analyzing, and reexamining the contents of the duffle bag. Along with examination came speculation, extrapolation, and pondering. Still, no definite conclusions had been reached. There wasn't enough evidence to decide, for certain, that Joshua Howard was a Fury Follower, or that he'd killed Ivan Volkov.

The items from Joshua's duffle bag seemed to corroborate Octavia's belief that Joshua was the "better suspect" who'd killed Ivan Volkov. Beanie had been quick to dismiss the attorney's accusations, which were based on the unreliable memory of a deranged, mentally ill woman prone to violent attacks. But the 3-by-5 notebook and the letter had forced him to reconcile things that didn't make sense. Things that couldn't be true. Joshua was a Fury follower? How could that be? How could the intern be a killer?

Beanie sighed. Last night, after he and Noelle had put the boys to bed, he'd picked his wife's brain about the conundrum. Again. He'd shared the revelations about Joshua with Noelle the same day he'd met with Friday. She'd been fascinated but unable to provide any insight.

Reaching toward his plastic inbox/outbox tray, Beanie picked up the letter written to The Fury.

He still struggled to believe the words. The sentences that chilled him. The paragraphs that horrified and intrigued him. Again, Beanie read the letter, trying to wrap his head around the pleading, adoring message.

Hello,

I hope this letter finds you well.

Despite your silence, which is more than I deserve, I must continue to entreat you and pray that you will grant me an audience as I so desperately need to speak with you and explain my deplorable actions against you. In my previous letters, I have apologized, but I fear mere words on paper are not enough and no excuse. I must see you in person. I hope you can find it in your heart to permit me so that I may give you the proper deference, respect, and worship that you deserve.

It was never my intention to betray you. I hate myself for my transgressions against you. I sinned and ruined your trust and faith in me! But I am prepared to make things right. I am prepared to offer you a sacrifice if you will allow me to do so.

Please, please, forgive me. After all these years, I now understand how selfish and foolish I was, and I repent to you for the error of my ways.

As always and forever, I remain

Your faithful follower

Sighing, Beanie read the letter once again, and then returned it to the plastic tray.

Something about the letter bothered him. And it wasn't the tribulating and lamenting about transgressions and betrayal. He couldn't quite put his finger on what bothered him. Somehow the letter seemed … he wasn't sure, but all he could think was that—

"So, I think I have proof that Joshua is, in fact, a Fury follower," said Stevie as he sank into the chair in front of Beanie's desk.

Startled from his thoughts, Beanie asked, "What kind of proof?"

"So, you asked me to see if my cousin could get into Joshua's laptop," began Stevie.

"Did your cousin find anything?" asked Beanie, hoping Stevie's hacker cousin, an elusive person no one at the paper had met or knew much about, had uncovered information about Joshua Howard.

Stevie said, "Turns out, Joshua was working on a podcast called 'Follow the Monster.'"

Beanie frowned. "What is the podcast about?"

"The Fury," said Stevie.

Beanie's pulse jumped. "A podcast about the Fury?"

"Well, technically, the podcast is about followers of the Fury," said Stevie. "My cousin found podcast notes and raw, unedited audio files of the podcast outtakes. He made copies. Let me email them to you so we can hear what Joshua has to say."

27

Minutes later, Beanie opened the first .mpeg file, named 'How I found the follower', and increased the volume on his computer.

Beanie leaned back in his chair as Joshua's voice began: "I found the Fury follower by chance. It was fate. Happenstance. That's how I'll start this episode of the podcast. Pretty good start. Then, I'll talk about how I changed shifts with a co-worker and then saw a package addressed to the prison at the Russian couple's house. The package was addressed to the Fury, but it used his real name, and it made me wonder. So I confronted the Russians. They said they hadn't sent the package. Claimed they didn't know The Fury. Of course, I didn't believe them. The wife accused me of putting the packages on their porch, which was crazy. She even attacked me. Lunged at me and bit my shoulder. I didn't know what to think, except, did she really just bite me? The husband hustled her into the house then came back onto the porch with some alcohol and gauze. Guess he was gonna cleanse my wound. Yeah, I wanted more than a band-aid, which is what I told him, but that's not for the first episode. I'll talk about that later. Maybe in an episode I'll call The Russians. Anyway. Turns out, I was wrong. Turns out, the packages were being sent by the old guy. The Russians weren't the Fury followers. The old guy is the real Fury Follower. So, I made contact.

Told the old guy I was a Fury follower myself … yeah, so that's how the first podcast will go."

The file ended.

Stevie said, "Joshua is a Fury follower."

"Apparently," murmured Beanie, though he still wasn't convinced. "Unbelievable."

Beanie asked, "Did you catch when he said the packages to the Fury were being sent by the old guy? And that the old guy is the real Fury Follower? I'll bet he was talking about Rufus Mason."

"Why do you think that?" asked Stevie.

"Natalya Volkov claimed that Mason was a Fury follower," said Beanie. "Now Joshua Howard says the follower is an old guy. It's got to be Mason."

Stevie said, "Let's listen to the file named 'Meeting the follower.'"

Beanie opened the file, his heart slamming as Joshua's disembodied voice filled his small cubicle: "So, for episode two, I'll talk about meeting the Fury follower. The old guy. I think of him as the man who followed the monster to hell and back again … okay, that's a good line … the man who followed the monster, no, wait … instead, I'll say, the day I met the man who followed the monster to hell and back. Maybe. It's okay. Not the best. I could probably do better. Anyway. Need to remember that I can't say his name in the podcast, or he won't talk to me. Can't get the guy in trouble with the cops."

Beanie glanced at Stevie, who stared at him with a grave expression.

Joshua's voice continued: "Anyway, so I can talk about how I introduced myself to the old guy. Told him, Hi, my name is Joshua, and I'm just like you, a follower of the Fury. The old guy invited me in. I asked him about the packages to the Fury. He told me he made a mistake. Told me he'd sinned against the Fury. Said he'd killed a woman, cut her up, and buried her beneath a mango tree to impress the Fury. But the Fury wasn't impressed."

The filed ended.

Stevie said, "So the follower killed a woman and buried her beneath a mango tree? Isn't that what Mason supposedly did to his wife?"

Disquieted and ill at ease, Beanie said, "For years, the rumor about Mason has been that his wife didn't disappear. He killed her, dismembered her body, and buried her in his backyard. Can't believe it's true …"

Stevie said, "Let's listen to 'The Plan for Forgiveness.'"

Minutes later, Joshua's voice filled the small cubicle: "The old guy was really upset about sinning against the Fury. Kept saying he had to ask the Fury for forgiveness. Had to prove to the Fury that he was really repentant. The old man said he needed to give the Fury a sacrifice. Ivan Volkov. The old guy said Volkov knew things about him that he didn't think Volkov should know. Things about what that old guy had done. The old guy said he had a plan. We could kill Volkov. Do it together. Or I could kill Volkov because—"

Abruptly, the filed ended.

Beanie stared at Stevie. "What the …?"

His face grim, Stevie said, "Well, there's the proof. Joshua killed Ivan Volkov, just like his girlfriend suspected. And maybe Rufus Mason helped him."

Beanie rubbed his jaw. "I don't think so …"

"What do you mean?"

"I don't think Joshua killed Ivan Volkov," said Beanie.

"But he just said he did," said Stevie. "You heard the audio."

Glancing at Stevie, Beanie said, "I heard him say that the old guy came up with a plan to kill Volkov."

"Or, that they could kill Volkov together," pointed out Stevie. "Or Joshua could kill Volkov."

"Right. Joshua *could* kill Volkov," clarified Beanie. "Joshua doesn't confess to killing Volkov. Or, even agreeing to help the old guy—who I'm sure is Rufus Mason—kill Volkov."

Stevie said, "Well, the audio cut out before Joshua could confess. And, you know, when you think about it, why would Joshua confess to killing Volkov? And if he killed Volkov, why would he cop to planning the murder? How do we even know that there is an old guy? Joshua could have made that up."

"Why would he have made up the old guy?" asked Beanie.

"Maybe he was creating a false suspect for the cops," said Stevie. "He's a Fury follower, and he plans to kill Volkov, so he knows the cops will investigate the murder. He also knows he might become a person of interest because he's got beef with the Volkovs. So, he decides to concoct this story about meeting a Fury follower who supposedly wanted to kill Ivan Volkov."

"Let's say you're right," said Beanie, though he thought Stevie was completely off base. "If Joshua tells the cops about the old guy who wanted to kill Volkov, then the cops will want him to identify that guy. Is he going to lie and tell the cops that the old guy is Rufus Mason?"

Stevie nodded. "Probably."

Beanie said, "But, then the cops would question Rufus Mason. They would determine that he didn't kill Volkov."

"Possibly," allowed Stevie. "But what if Joshua made sure that there was enough evidence against Mason to convince the police that Mason killed Volkov."

Frowning, Beanie said, "So, you think Joshua planned to frame Mason for Volkov's murder? You really think he's that diabolical?"

"You really think Joshua is completely innocent?" challenged Stevie.

Looking away, Beanie pondered the question. He wasn't sure how to answer it. Not yet. Wasn't sure he wanted to answer the question. Though it bothered him, Beanie couldn't deny that the intern was a Fury follower. The notebook, the letter to the Fury, and the podcast audio proved Joshua's sick obsession with the serial killer. Or, at least, it seemed to. Nothing had been authenticated yet, but how could he dismiss the evidence? Still, Beanie struggled to think of Joshua as Machiavellian and murderous.

"Anyway," said Stevie, standing. "Vivian needs to hear these audio files."

"Email them to her," said Beanie. "I'll meet you in her office after I get another cup of coffee."

Nodding, Stevie headed back to his cubicle. Beanie drug a hand down his face, feeling as though he'd been sucker-punched and was struggling to breathe.

The information on Joshua's podcast files had hit him like a sledgehammer. While Stevie had focused on Joshua's possible involvement in the death of Ivan Volkov, Beanie preferred to concentrate on the old guy. The Fury follower Joshua had discovered was sending packages to the Fury. Rufus Mason, thought Beanie, his mind conjuring an image of the pallid, skeletal man. He wasn't quite sure how to wrap his head around the fact that a Fury follower lived five houses away from him. He couldn't believe the rumors about Rufus Mason were true.

Shuddering, Beanie let out a breath. He wasn't sure what to think about Mason, but he was sure about one thing. Joshua hadn't killed Ivan Volkov. Maybe the intern was a Fury follower, and that was horrible and sickening, but the affable redhead with the infectious grin hadn't stabbed a man to death.

Beanie rubbed his jaw. Part of him wasn't even sure about Joshua being a Fury follower.

Despite the bombshell revelations on the audio files, Beanie felt there was something weird about Joshua's commentary. He couldn't put his finger on what he found odd about the podcast notes, but he had a feeling there was more to the story. Or maybe he didn't fully understand the story. Or, possibly, what he thought was the story was actually … what?

Beanie stood. He didn't know what to think.

Except maybe that he really needed that cup of coffee.

28

"Leo listened to Joshua's podcast files this morning," said Vivian, tapping her red editing pen against her cheek.

Sitting in the chair in front of his boss's desk, Beanie took a sip of coffee. At an hour before four in the afternoon, he'd been thinking of a third cup of coffee when Vivian buzzed him, requesting that he come to her office.

He wasn't surprised that she wanted to discuss Joshua's podcast audio files.

After he and Stevie had listened to the audio yesterday, they'd met with Vivian, who'd also listened. The podcast audio was astonishing and intriguing, she'd agreed, but she wanted them to hold off on writing an article about the revelations. Vivian explained that she needed to allow Leo the chance to evaluate the shocking evidence.

"What did he think?" asked Beanie.

"He agrees that the files are explosive," said Vivian. "Combined with Joshua's notebook and the letter to the Fury, Leo believes it's a story that needs to be told. However, the evidence has to be authenticated before we publish the story. We need to make sure that Joshua Howard wrote those entries in that notebook. We need proof that Joshua recorded those audio files."

Nodding, Beanie said, "Makes sense."

Beanie thought the guy he'd heard on the podcast files sounded like Joshua, but he couldn't swear that it was really the intern. Audio was usually inadmissible because it was difficult to authenticate.

"And, of course, we have to consider whether, or not, we want to share this information with the St. Killian Police Department," said Vivian. "Leo talked to the Bronson Publishing lawyers and, of course, we don't have to tell the cops what we know. We aren't legally obligated to give evidence to the police. The Palmchat Islands does have shield laws designed to protect reporter's privilege."

Beanie took another sip of coffee. He'd taken a class about reporter's privilege and the rights of journalists in college. The *Palmchat Gazette* couldn't be compelled to hand over information to the police. But that didn't mean a prosecutor wouldn't file a motion to force compliance if the cops found out they had crucial evidence connected to a murder investigation.

"The question is, do we have a moral obligation to share this information?" asked Vivian, rocking back in her leather chair.

Rubbing his jaw, Beanie asked, "What does Leo think about that?"

Her smile wry, Vivian said, "Leo believes that the police should know about the notebook, the letter to the Fury, and the audio files. But ... not until *after* we've published the story first."

Unease settling within him, Beanie took another sip of coffee. He wasn't sure about giving the information to the police. Considering that he wasn't convinced the evidence against Joshua was credible, he was reluctant to inform the cops about the podcast audio. However, he did believe the police should know about Rufus Mason, the old man Joshua had referenced in the files.

Before drifting to sleep last night, Beanie had ruminated on the podcast audio, turning it over and over in his mind. He'd concluded that Stevie was wrong. Joshua hadn't killed Volkov. Mason, the Fury follower, had killed the Russian. Mason had come up with the plan. Mason had wanted Volkov dead because the Russian knew something about him. Beanie recalled that Natalya had said Mason threatened to kill Ivan. Mason had the motive for murder. Not Joshua.

As for writing the story, Beanie wasn't keen about that either, considering it would probably be slanted to paint Joshua in a negative light. He didn't want to write an article suggesting that Joshua was a murdering Fury follower. But maybe he wouldn't have to, especially since it would be next to impossible to verify the information Friday had given them. Not that he wanted to verify the evidence. Beanie wasn't anxious to confirm Joshua's involvement in Ivan Volkov's death.

"Speaking of explosive evidence," said Vivian. "One of my sources at the St. Killian police department, who shall remain nameless, told me that the case against Natalya Volkov is starting to collapse."

Beanie stared at Vivian. "Are you serious?"

"Forensic testing confirmed that the saliva found in Ivan Volkov's bite wounds wasn't a match for Natalya Volkov."

"So Natalya didn't bite her husband?" asked Beanie.

"And there's something else she might not have done," said Vivian.

An odd chill passed through Beanie. "What do you mean?"

"The police believe they recovered the knife Natalya brandished in the Mendez surveillance video," said Vivian. "They found it in the back of the Volkov's car. Natalya's prints were on that knife, but—"

"Wait a minute," interrupted Beanie. "How was the knife found in the back of the Volkov's car? The knife was located beneath Ivan's body in the jungle."

"Exactly," said Vivian. "I was about to tell you that the knife Natalya had in that video is not the murder weapon. In fact, Natalya's prints aren't on the knife that killed Ivan."

"That doesn't mean Natalya didn't kill her husband," said Beanie, reluctant to abandon his suspicions of the widow.

Tilting her head, Vivian said, "What if I told you that a man bit Ivan Volkov?"

"What?" Beanie asked, shocked.

"The DNA in the saliva was male," said Vivian.

Beanie took a quick sip of the lukewarm coffee.

"The cops are seriously exploring the idea that Ivan Volkov was killed by a man," said Vivian. "And maybe you should, too."

"You mean, maybe I should start considering that Joshua killed Ivan?"

Vivian sighed. "Listen, I don't want to think that Joshua could be a murderer. But we have to think about the evidence. The notebook. The letter to the Fury—"

"Evidence that may or may not be real," said Beanie. "You said yourself that we need to authenticate everything before we publish anything."

Tapping her red editing pen against the edge of her desk, Vivian said, "There's something else I need to tell you."

Wary, Beanie asked, "Do I need another cup of coffee?"

Vivian said, "The forensic pathologist found white hibiscus petals in Ivan Volkov's throat."

"White hibiscus petals?"

Her expression darkened, Vivian said, "That's a hallmark of a Fury follower."

Confused, Beanie said, "I thought the Fury used blue hibiscus as his signature."

Nodding, Vivian said, "He did. But his followers use white hibiscus."

A memory sparked within Beanie. Something about a white hibiscus. Why did he remember a white hibiscus? Had he seen one recently?

Vivian said, "So the police are looking at the possibility that Ivan Volkov was killed by a Fury follower."

Back at this desk, Beanie reflected on the new developments in the Ivan Volkov case, which Vivian wanted him to detail in his next story about the Jungle Corpse Murder.

Staring at his computer, Beanie hesitated to begin the first draft. The new information was disturbing, and it cast serious doubts on Natalya Volkov as the murderer of her husband. Beanie had convinced himself that Natalya was a killer, even in the absence of any physical evidence connecting her to the murder, because of Mendez's surveillance video and Natalya's past violent behavior, which he'd experienced firsthand.

Maintaining his belief in Natalya's guilt was difficult now that he knew the widow's prints didn't match those on the murder weapon and that a man had bitten Ivan Volkov. The white hibiscus petals found in Ivan's throat had thrown Beanie for a loop. He wasn't surprised the cops no longer liked the widow as the killer.

There was hardly any evidence connecting Natalya to Ivan's murder.

Unfortunately, there was evidence connecting Joshua to Ivan Volkov's death. The 3-by-5 notebook detailing his plans to target and take down Volkov. The disturbing letter to the Fury. The podcast audio. And yet, despite how incriminating the evidence against the intern seemed, Beanie wasn't convinced that any of it proved Joshua's guilt. He wasn't sure the evidence was even authentic.

But if the evidence was real, then it implicated Rufus Mason—the old guy—more than it did Joshua, in Beanie's opinion. Mason, the Fury follower, had threatened to kill Ivan.

Sitting back in his leather chair, Beanie stared at the ceiling tiles. His thoughts returned to the white hibiscus petals in Volkov's throat. Beanie had researched Fury followers in the past and remembered that they often bit their victims in homage to the cannibalistic serial killer. Ivan Volkov's bite wounds made sense if his killer was a Fury follower. A male Fury follower.

Like Rufus Mason.

Or Joshua, a small voice Beanie couldn't ignore whispered in his head.

Beanie's stomach lurched as Joshua's notebook and letter to the Fury flooded his mind. The intern's own words indicted him as a Fury follower who'd stalked Ivan Volkov to kill him. And yet Beanie had a hard time believing that Joshua was a murderer. The young man he'd mentored and gotten to know couldn't be a Fury follower. Didn't make sense. Didn't seem possible. Beanie was biased because of his relationship with the intern, but he had to believe he was a better judge of character. How was it possible that Joshua had fooled him? How was it possible that he'd mentored a murderer?

Beanie's desk phone rang.

Relieved for the chance to focus on anything else, he picked up the phone. "Roland Bean."

"Hey, it's Fields," said the St. Killian officer. "Got a minute?"

"Sure. What's up?"

"I need to find Joshua Howard," said Fields. "Have you heard from him?

We've been trying to reach him, but he's not answering calls or responding to texts."

"He hasn't responded to any of my calls or texts, either," said Beanie. "I haven't heard from him since the video call."

"Well, if you hear from him," said Fields, "will you give me a call?"

Disturbed by the tension in the officer's tone, Beanie asked, "What's going on?"

"DNA from the saliva found in Ivan Volkov's bite wounds is a match for the DNA found in the saliva of Joshua Howard's finger," said Fields.

"The same person bit Ivan Volkov and Joshua Howard?" asked Beanie, recalling the information Vivian had received from her confidential source.

"The same guy bit Joshua and Ivan Volkov," said Fields. "But, that's not why I need to find Joshua. While forensics was testing the saliva found in Joshua's finger, they scraped the fingernail. They found microscopic residue which they tested, and which turned out to be petals from a white hibiscus flower."

Beanie's pulse jumped. "What does that mean?"

Fields said, "I don't think I told you this, but the pathologist found crushed hibiscus petals in Ivan Volkov's throat. The forensics report suggested that Joshua Howard had stuffed those white hibiscus petals into Volkov's throat. The detectives started to wonder if Joshua might have killed Volkov, so they ran Joshua's prints against the prints on the murder weapon."

"And?" asked Beanie, his heart pounding.

Fields said, "And prints came back as a match for Joshua Howard."

29

"Vivian and Leo are going to give the evidence against Joshua to the St. Killian cops," said Beanie as he sat down on the side of the king-sized bed he shared with his wife.

Sitting in the armchair across from the bed, Noelle frowned. "That's a good thing, right? The cops need to know that Joshua is a Fury follower, and he killed Ivan Volkov."

Massaging the back of his neck, Beanie said, "After Fields told me that Joshua's prints were found on the knife that killed Volkov, Vivian figured we needed to show the police the notebook and the letter to the Fury, but …"

"But what?"

"But is Joshua really a Fury follower?" asked Beanie. "Did he kill Ivan Volkov?"

"Don't tell me you think Joshua is innocent?" Noelle shook her head. "His prints were on the murder weapon. And white hibiscus residue was found beneath Joshua's finger. And don't forget about the notebook. And the letter to the Fury. And the podcast audio."

"There's no proof that Joshua wrote any of those notebook entries or the letter," said Beanie. "No proof that he recorded the audio."

"You said it sounded like him," Noelle said.

"Yeah, it did."

"So now you think it wasn't Joshua?" asked Noelle. "You think it was someone mimicking his voice?"

"I do think Joshua recorded the audio," said Beanie. "I don't believe he was telling the truth."

"Why would he lie about being a Fury follower?" asked Noelle.

"That's what doesn't make any sense," said Beanie.

His wife stood and then walked to the bed. Sitting next to Beanie, she said, "Roland, I know how disappointing finding out the truth about Joshua has been for you. And disappointing is an understatement. I know you really liked Joshua. You liked mentoring him. It's got to be heartbreaking to know that you were so wrong about him."

"But am I wrong about him?" asked Beanie. "What's disappointing is that I wasn't able to authenticate any of the evidence against Joshua that Friday gave me. Friday said she recognized the notebook entries as Joshua's handwriting, but a handwriting expert needs to establish that."

"I'm sure the police will do that," said Noelle.

"It's not just the notebook," said Beanie. "It's also the letter to the Fury. The way it's written is weird. The phrasing, I mean. Joshua is a twenty-two-year-old kid. And the letter is very anachronistic in the structure and word choice."

"Well, the Fury is in his seventies, right?" asked Noelle as she moved to stretch out on the bed. "Maybe Joshua was, in his own sick, twisted way, trying to be respectful to the Fury, or something."

Beanie exhaled. "Okay, well, in terms of the audio … it sounds fake."

"Fake?" echoed Noelle.

Nodding, Beanie said, "Like he's acting. Or pretending to be a Fury follower."

"But why would he do that?"

"I don't know," said Beanie, stretching out next to his wife. "I just … I don't like the idea of giving that evidence to the cops. I don't want to get Joshua in trouble for something he didn't do."

"I'm sure the cops will vet the evidence," assured Noelle. "If it's all fake, they'll be able to figure it out. But, Roland, the evidence Friday gave you isn't going to cause any more trouble for him than the murder weapon with his prints on it."

Nodding, Beanie said, "I know that, babe, but—"

"But you need to come to terms with the fact that Joshua killed Ivan Volkov," said Noelle. "He's a Fury follower and a murderer, and he needs to be caught before he kills again."

30

STUDENT CHARGED IN ISLAND CORPSE MURDER

Staring at his computer, Beanie skimmed the story, written three days ago. The collaboration with Stevie was still trending. Currently, it was the most popular story on the paper's website.

Beanie was glad for the success, but something about the story still bothered him. The article outlined the compelling physical evidence against the intern, leading to an obvious conclusion—Joshua Howard killed Ivan Volkov.

Attempting to cast doubt on Joshua's guilt, Beanie had written two paragraphs about a potential alternate suspect—the old guy. With no concrete evidence of the old guy's true identity, Beanie hadn't been able to out Rufus Mason. However, he'd tried to make a strong case, stating that an anonymous source had provided information about an old Fury follower who'd wanted Ivan Volkov dead. He doubted the readers were convinced. After all, Joshua's prints, not the unknown old guy's, had been found on the murder weapon.

Rubbing his jaw, Beanie sighed as familiar questions haunted him. Was Joshua really a Fury follower? Had he killed Ivan Volkov? Beanie didn't know, but he didn't think so, and he didn't know why Friday's evidence against Joshua didn't convince him.

Beanie supposed that evidence would have convinced the paper's readers—if they'd been privy to it.

Vivian had decided not to publish the 3-by-5 spiral journal, the letter to the Fury, and the audio files. She didn't want to print any details they couldn't conclusively verify. And, as it turned out, the cops weren't necessarily convinced by Friday's evidence. The detectives had decided to arrest Joshua solely because of his prints on the murder weapon and the white hibiscus petal residue beneath Joshua's finger. The police also weren't moved by Beanie's theory that "the old guy" had killed Volkov.

During the meeting with the St. Killian detectives, in which the evidence from Joshua's duffel bag was handed over to the cops, Beanie had brought up "the old guy." Sharing his belief that "the old guy" was Rufus Mason, Beanie explained how Mason had a better motive to kill Ivan Volkov. He'd pointed out that Mason had threatened to kill Volkov. The detectives admitted to investigating Natalya's claim, though they declined to share the results of their investigation into Mason. Beanie suspected, however, that they hadn't been able to verify Natalya's assertion. In the end, the detectives weren't interested in Beanie's speculation and conjecture, not when they had latent prints on the murder weapon.

As a result, he and Stevie had to put forth a theory that Joshua had targeted Volkov because the Russian had refused to compensate him for injuries Joshua had sustained following Natalya's attack.

After a sip of his second cup of coffee, Beanie tried to determine why he didn't think Joshua had killed Volkov. Opening a Word document, he began typing his thoughts.

The story of Joshua Howard had been strange and convoluted from the very beginning, when Beanie discovered the student's finger in Ethan's candy pail. Initially, Beanie thought the finger had been cut off, but he'd learned it had been bitten off. But who had done it? Beanie had no idea. Joshua hadn't wanted to talk about the gruesome injury.

Joshua's girlfriend had made matters worse, at first. Influenced by a psychological thriller novel, she was convinced Joshua had been killed. Or maybe missing. But Joshua had never been missing. Beanie had talked to the enigmatic intern. Sure, it hadn't been much of a conversation, but it proved Friday wrong.

Beanie took another sip of coffee. Things had gotten crazier when Joshua's connection to the Volkovs had been exposed. An unresolved lawsuit, a failed mediation, and stalking had led to the most explosive revelation.

Joshua Howard was a Fury Follower who'd killed Ivan Volkov.

But was that really true?

Joshua's prints were on the knife used to kill Volkov, and it was hard to argue with that. In the audio files, Joshua had talked about killing Volkov. He must have made good on that threat. The entries in the notebook suggested that Joshua was targeting Volkov. That Joshua wanted to take the man down. Put him in the dirt. And the letter to the Fury was beyond bizarre. Beanie struggled to process it...

Maybe that was the problem, Beanie thought.

The inconclusive evidence bothered Beanie. The things they hadn't been able to prove gave him doubts. Had Joshua written the entries in the spiral notebook? Had he typed the letter to the Fury? Had he made the podcast audio files?

Maybe, he had, but Beanie wasn't sure about that.

The St. Killian Police Department was sure, however.

They'd issued an arrest warrant for Joshua after officially charging him with the murder of Ivan Volkov. Currently, the police had no idea of Joshua's location and had instituted an island-wide search.

With help from Stevie, Beanie had written, POLICE HUNT STUDENT ACCUSED OF JUNGLE CORPSE MURDER.

The popular article had already spawned several supposed sightings of Joshua. Beanie, however, was disappointed, but not shocked, when he'd surveyed the comments, which had pivoted from support for Joshua to scorn toward the intern. Readers and residents who had formerly been worried about him were now on the warpath, organizing search parties to locate the intern and bring him to justice.

Beanie rubbed his eyes. He still struggled to believe that the intern had killed Ivan Volkov, despite the physical evidence against him. Beanie couldn't explain away Joshua's prints on the murder weapon. But the intern's prints on the knife didn't automatically mean Joshua had stabbed Volkov.

There was another possibility, though he was reluctant to share it with anyone.

Beanie suspected that Joshua was being set up—by Rufus Mason.

After learning about the white hibiscus petals found in Volkov's throat, Beanie had ruminated on the detail, turning it over and over in his mind. When Vivian had first mentioned it, the white hibiscus had sparked a memory he couldn't recall at the time.

Now he realized why the flower had seemed so familiar. Not because of its association with the Fury followers. But, because of Rufus Mason. Noelle had seen Mason buying a white hibiscus at the nursery. He'd checked with his wife, and Noelle confirmed she'd seen Mason buying the flower weeks before Ivan Volkov's murder.

Mason might have crushed those white petals and stuffed them down Volkov's throat. Mason was the old Fury follower Joshua talked about on his podcast audio files. The old man who'd killed his wife and buried her in the backyard. The old man desperate for the Fury's forgiveness.

Rufus Mason, Beanie believed, was Ivan Volkov's killer. Octavia Constant had named him as a "better suspect" based on Natalya's claims that she'd heard him threaten to kill her husband. At the time, Beanie had dismissed Natalya's story as the paranoid ramblings of a depraved lunatic, but Natalya had been telling the truth.

And it made sense that Mason had killed Volkov, thought Beanie. As a Fury follower, the man would bite his victim, in deference to the Fury, before killing him. And the DNA in Volkov's bite wounds was male.

More importantly, the DNA in the saliva found in Joshua's finger was male. And it was the same DNA that had been found in Ivan's wounds. The same male who'd bitten off Joshua's finger had bitten Volkov. Had to be Mason, reasoned Beanie.

Beanie's cell phone rang. Beanie glanced at the number. ZELLER, WALTER, DR. Curious about why the psychologist might be calling him, Beanie answered. "Roland Bean."

"Mr. Bean, this is Dr. Walter Zeller," he said. "Are you available to meet this evening, perhaps around six? At my home?"

"About what?" asked Beanie.

"About Rufus Mason," said Zeller.

"What about Mason?" asked Beanie. "Can't you tell me now?"

"I'm driving, and it's better if we speak in person," said Zeller. "Are you available?"

Frustrated by Zeller's evasiveness, Beanie was nevertheless curious. "Fine," said Beanie. "I'll see you at six."

31

Standing on Dr. Walter Zeller's porch, Beanie hesitated.

He glanced at his watch. Two minutes to six, when he was scheduled to meet with the psychologist who wanted to discuss Rufus Mason. Beanie exhaled. He wasn't sure it was a good idea to meet with Zeller, but he wanted to find out what the man knew. Especially if the information supported Beanie's belief that Mason had killed Ivan Volkov.

Raising his hand, Beanie knocked against the wooden door and—

The door was already open, slightly ajar.

His hackles rising, Beanie pushed the door, allowing it to swing back.

Peering into the dim foyer, Beanie called out, "Dr. Zeller? Are you home? It's Roland Bean ..."

Silence from inside the foyer.

Fighting his apprehension, and maybe his common sense, Beanie stepped over the threshold into the house. Glancing around the foyer, he saw nothing amiss, and continued, looking over his shoulder back at the opened door from time to time. Beanie wasn't sure if he wanted to make sure that the door remained open, or if he wanted to turn around and take off running toward it.

His heart was slamming, but Beanie told himself to think calmly. Rationally. Just because a door was ajar didn't necessarily mean anything bad had happened. Could have been that Zeller didn't realize he hadn't closed the door all the way?

Beanie made his way into the living room, looking around. Again, he saw nothing out of place.

"Dr. Zeller?" he called out, hoping the man wasn't playing some weird game with him. But why would he? Well, Zeller was a psychologist. Maybe he was conducting some psychological test? But why?

Looking toward the kitchen, Beanie saw appliances gleaming in the late afternoon sun streaming through the window over the sink. The countertops were bare and clean.

Taking another breath, Beanie headed down the hall leading to Zeller's office. His apprehension fading, he thought maybe that Zeller had left the house, for some reason, and hadn't made sure the door was shut on his way out.

Facing the door to Zeller's office, which was half-opened, Beanie knocked on the door. "Dr. Zeller?"

Beanie pushed the door open, and—

"What the ...?"

Zeller's office looked as though a Cat-5 hurricane had blown through it. Books and papers were strewn and littered across the floor. One of the chairs in front of Zeller's desk was overturned, and the other had been smashed to pieces. The curtains hanging from the large window had been pulled down to the floor where they lay in shredded strips.

As Beanie surveyed the room, his head whipping left and right, eyes darting, his gaze alighted on a lone arm lying prone, extending from behind the desk.

"Dr. Zeller!" Beanie crossed the room, stepping over the debris.

Behind the desk, he saw the psychologist on the floor, lying on his back. Swallowing bile, Beanie resisted the urge to flee as he stared at the doctor. Zeller's chest looked as though a wild animal, something with razor-sharp claws, had ripped it open.

Beanie struggled to breathe. Pushing aside his terror and ignoring his twisting stomach, Beanie leaned next to the man. "Dr. Zeller? Can you hear me? It's Roland Bean. Let me—"

"Mason," Zeller sputtered, coughing blood. "Fury ... follower ..."

"Don't try to talk, okay?" said Beanie, kneeling next to Zeller's body. "I'm going to call an ambulance!"

"Fury follower …" Zeller wheezed, his bloody chest rising and falling rapidly. "Mason … killed … "

"Dr. Zeller, please!" Beanie said, trying to stay calm. "Listen to me … you need to get to the hospital immediately! I'm calling an ambulance!"

"Mason … Fury!" screeched Dr. Zeller, grabbing Beanie's arm. "Mason … Fury … follower!"

On his feet, Beanie thrust a shaking hand into his pocket and pulled out his cell phone.

32

"Have you heard anything new about Dr. Zeller's condition?" asked Noelle.

Pacing at the foot of their king-sized bed, Beanie looked at his wife, lounging on the duvet, giving him a concerned stare. After dinner with their boys, they'd given the little guys baths, then read them their favorite books before putting them to bed.

"As far as I know, he made it out of surgery," Beanie said. "Haven't heard anything other than that."

Several days had passed since Beanie had found Dr. Walter Zeller near death in his ransacked office. He'd called an ambulance, and the EMTs arrived quickly and whisked Zeller away to St. Killian General Hospital. As cops and other first responders converged on the crime scene, Beanie had been herded into the foyer, where he was told to wait until the detectives arrived to take his statement.

"Can't believe what happened to him," said Noelle. "Do the cops have any suspects?"

Beanie stopped pacing and looked at the ceiling. "Fields says they've just started the investigation, but ..."

"But what?" asked Noelle.

"Zeller was viciously attacked," said Beanie. "Reminds me of what happened to Ivan Volkov. Someone tore him apart, too."

"Joshua Howard," said Noelle.

Beanie shook his head. "But Joshua didn't attack Dr. Zeller. It was Rufus Mason."

"You think Mason attacked Dr. Zeller? Why?" asked Noelle. "Because Zeller told you that Mason is a Fury follower?"

"I already suspected Mason was a Fury follower from what I heard on Joshua's podcast files," said Beanie, joining his wife on the bed. "I think Mason attacked Dr. Zeller because the man had information to prove that Mason framed Joshua for Ivan Volkov's murder."

"You think Mason framed Joshua?" asked Noelle. "Babe, I don't know about that. Makes more sense that Joshua and Mason were working together, considering what you heard on Joshua's podcast files. Didn't Joshua suggest that he and Mason could kill Ivan together? Maybe they tried to kill Dr. Zeller together? Because Dr. Zeller wanted to talk to you about Mason. Maybe Dr. Zeller had some evidence against Mason *and* Joshua."

"I don't think that's true," said Beanie, joining his wife on the bed. "I don't think Joshua is a Fury follower working with Mason. I don't think Joshua killed Ivan—"

"But Joshua's prints were on the knife used to kill Ivan," said Noelle. "Joshua also confessed that he's a Fury follower."

"I know that," began Beanie, readjusting the pillows behind him.

"But you don't believe it," said Noelle.

"I'm having a hard time," admitted Beanie, rubbing his hand across the back of his neck.

Shaking her head, Noelle asked, "Why? I don't understand."

"Because I know Joshua," said Beanie. "It doesn't make sense that he's a Fury follower."

"Roland, listen," began Noelle, moving closer to Beanie. "I know you consider yourself to be a good judge of character, and finding out the truth about Joshua has been really disheartening for you. Joshua lied to you. He completely misrepresented himself."

"I have every reason to feel like Joshua made a fool of me." Beanie put an arm around Noelle and pulled her close to him. "Turns out there was a lot I didn't know about him, and maybe one of those things happens to be that he's a Fury follower. But I don't think he killed Volkov."

"Okay, I'll humor you," said Noelle. "How do you think Mason set up Joshua?"

As his wife snuggled next to him, Beanie said, "Honestly, I think Joshua got caught up with Mason. He wanted to do this podcast about Fury followers. Then he finds an actual Fury follower. Rufus Mason. An experienced Fury follower who was probably grooming him, acting as a mentor, actually. So Mason finds out that he and Joshua had a common foe."

"Ivan Volkov," said Noelle.

Nodding, Beanie said, "So Rufus Mason suggests that he and Joshua get rid of Ivan."

"Which they do," said Noelle.

"Or, maybe they don't," said Beanie. "What I mean is, Joshua might have agreed to help Mason, but what if he got scared? What if he backed out? Realized that he was in way over his head?"

Noelle sighed. "I guess I could see something like that happening. Sometimes, the fantasy is more enticing and interesting than the reality of something."

"Exactly," said Beanie. "So, Joshua decides he can't go through with helping Mason kill Ivan Volkov. Mason gets upset. He probably thinks that Joshua isn't faithful enough to be a Fury follower, so he wants to punish him. Or get back at him for not being willing to kill for the Fury."

"And then what?"

"And then Mason manufactures a bunch of evidence against Joshua," said Beanie. "The two of them obviously spent time together, so it would have been possible for Joshua to pick up the knife that Mason used to kill Volkov."

"Maybe," conceded Noelle. "I guess it could have happened that way, but ..."

"But, I think I know what you're going to say," said Beanie. "How do I prove that Mason framed Joshua? And, I have to admit that I really don't know ..."

33

"Got some news about Dr. Walter Zeller," said Officer Damon Fields.

"Good news or bad news?" asked Beanie as he pressed the 'speaker' button on his desk phone. Turning to his computer, he opened a Word file.

A week had passed since the vicious attack on Dr. Zeller, who'd survived the surgery, but remained in a medically induced coma, and was unable to tell the police who had attacked him.

Beanie's story, RETIRED DOCTOR LEFT FOR DEAD, had been enormously popular. Though the article focused on the gruesome assault, it also reminded readers of the connection between Ivan Volkov and Dr. Zeller and provided details on the similarities between Zeller's horrible wounds and Volkov's mangled corpse.

Beanie's account suggested that Dr. Zeller had been attacked by Rufus Mason, whose name the retired psychologist had gasped before passing out. The story also informed readers that Mason had fled his home before the police could question him. Though he believed Mason had targeted Zeller because the doctor had learned about Mason's plot to frame Joshua for the murder of Ivan Volkov, Beanie had left his theories out of the article, at the request of Vivian, who didn't necessarily agree with his unfounded speculation.

"Interesting news," said Fields. "Medical reports show that Dr. Zeller had not only been stabbed but also bitten."

"Are you serious? Dr. Zeller was bitten?"

Fields said, "Bite wounds on his face and hands."

Beanie exhaled. "Wow ..."

"The saliva in Zeller's wounds was a match for the saliva we found in Ivan Volkov's wounds," said Fields, "and Joshua Howard's finger."

"So, whoever bit Joshua and Volkov also bit Zeller? Any idea who it is?"

"The detectives like Rufus Mason," said Fields. "They want to bring him in and get a DNA sample, but they have to find the guy first."

"He's still in the wind?" asked Beanie.

"Unfortunately," said Fields. "We were able to trace his financials. His American Express card shows a one-way flight to Spain."

"Why Spain?" asked Beanie.

"Spain doesn't have an extradition treaty with the Palmchat Islands," said Fields. "Also, the crime scene guys found bloody clothes in Mason's washing machine. And the blood on those clothes is a match for Zeller. So, this morning, we issued an arrest warrant for Mason for the attempted murder of Dr. Zeller."

"Do the detectives like Mason for the murder of Volkov?" asked Beanie, typing notes into his file.

"They like Joshua Howard," said Fields. "I know that's not what you want to hear, but Howard's prints are on the murder weapon and—"

"I know that, but ..."

"But what?" prompted Fields.

Beanie hesitated, reluctant to share his theory that Mason was framing Joshua. His wife and his coworkers had already shot down his theory. He didn't need Fields to tell him why he was stupid for believing in Joshua's innocence. Didn't need the overwhelming evidence against Joshua pointed out to him again.

Instead, Beanie said, "I have a question about the hibiscus petals beneath Joshua's finger. Noelle and I found the finger *before* Ivan was killed. Why would there be hibiscus petal residue beneath Joshua's nail before he murdered Ivan?"

"We're aware of that fact," said Fields. "The detectives think Joshua picked the flowers or crushed the petals before his finger was bitten off."

"About a week passed between the time Joshua's finger was found and when Ivan was killed," said Beanie. "Forensics really believes that Joshua prepared the petals a week in advance?"

"Apparently, the white hibiscus petals are an important part of the ritual when you kill for the Fury," said Fields. "So, it's possible Joshua bought the white hibiscus or grew it, or whatever before he decided to kill Volkov."

"Thanks for the information," said Beanie, recalling how Noelle had told him about Mason buying the white hibiscus from the nursery. Proof, in Beanie's estimation, that Mason could have crammed the white petals down Volkov's throat, but he doubted he could convince Fields to consider his theory.

After Beanie hung up with Fields, he stood and went to the breakroom for another cup of coffee. As he put a K-cup in the Keurig, Beanie reflected on the overwhelming evidence against the intern.

Evidence that was hard to defend or dispute. The intern's fingerprints on the murder weapon. White hibiscus petals beneath Joshua's finger, suggesting that the intern had crushed the hibiscus and shoved it down the Russian's throat. The notebook detailing how Joshua had stalked Ivan Volkov. How he'd wanted to take Volkov down and put him in the dirt. The podcast files where Joshua admitted to being a Fury follower.

Once his coffee was ready, Beanie added a little cream and sugar, then walked back to his cubicle.

Dropping down into his creaky leather chair, he took a sip of the steaming brew, ruminating on why the podcast audio bothered him. After listening to the files several more times during the week, he'd realized that Joshua sounded rehearsed. As though he was acting. Making up salacious details. Embellishing the truth.

Beanie recalled some of Joshua's assertions.

Told the old guy I was a follower myself.

Told him, Hi, my name is Joshua, and I'm just like you, a follower of the Fury.

But, just because Joshua had told Mason those things didn't mean he was telling the truth. Maybe he'd been trying to convince Mason to trust him so that Mason would open up about his experience as a Fury follower.

What better way to secure Mason's trust than to pretend they had something in common?

Back at his desk, Beanie ruminated on …

"You got a sec?"

"Sure," said Beanie. "What's up?"

"You still think Rufus Mason framed Joshua?" asked Stevie.

"You still think I'm crazy for thinking Mason framed Joshua?" asked Beanie.

"Actually, this is going to sound crazy, but I think you're right," said Stevie. "Not about Mason framing Joshua. About Joshua being framed."

"I'm not following you," said Beanie.

"I think you might be right. Joshua is being framed," said Stevie. "But not by Mason."

Beanie was confused. "Then, by who?"

"The old guy who buried a woman under the tree in his backyard," said Stevie.

"Rufus Mason," said Beanie. "The old man who killed his wife and—"

"No, that's not right …"

"What's not right?" asked Beanie.

"What you just said about the old man who killed his wife," said Stevie. "That's not what Joshua said about the old man."

"What did he say?"

"I printed out transcripts of the podcast audio files," Stevie said. "Joshua said the old man killed a woman and buried her under a tree. He didn't specifically say that the woman was the old man's wife."

"Are you serious?"

"I'll email you the transcripts," said Stevie. "And Joshua didn't name the Fury Follower. We all just assumed it was Rufus Mason. But what if it wasn't?"

Beanie stared at Stevie. "If Mason isn't the Fury follower, then who is?"

***

Nursing a third cup of coffee, Beanie sat at his desk, staring at the blank screen of his computer.

Several hours had passed since Stevie introduced the idea that the old man Joshua had referred to in his podcast audio files might not be Rufus Mason. Beanie had spent most of the afternoon trying to reconcile his suspicions and defend his theories in the face of conflicting evidence.

Rubbing his eyes, Beanie glanced at the clock in the lower right-hand corner of his computer screen.

6:14 p.m.

His productivity shot, Beanie decided to call it a night. He was tired of thinking about Mason and Joshua and the Fury and trying to make sense of the madness. What he need was a nice, frosty Felipe beer. A few sips of the island brew, and—

The desk phone rang.

Groaning, Beanie hesitated before picking up the receiver. Praying for a wrong number, he said, "Roland Bean."

"Roland, it's Anthony Mendez," said a smooth, suave baritone. "How are you?"

"Mr. Mendez, I was just about to leave the office, so—"

"This won't take but a minute," said Mendez. "I need some advice, and since you have a good relationship with the police, I figured you would be the best person to ask."

Confused, Beanie asked, "You need advice about the police?"

"I need to know if I should inform the police that I was wrong about some information I shared with them," said Mendez. "Will they accept my apology, do you think? Or will they be suspicious and accuse me of withholding information?"

"Probably will depend on the information you shared with them," said Beanie. "Is it about the Ivan Volkov murder?"

"It's about the Joshua Howard disappearance," said Mendez. "The student who wasn't missing. I gave the cops video of him going into the Volkov house the night he disappeared and told them that he didn't come out of the Volkov home; however, I was mistaken."

"You were mistaken?"

"Turns out Joshua did leave the Volkov house that night," said Mendez. "I found the video."

"Are you serious?"

"And you will never guess where he went afterward," said Mendez. "But, before you guess, I must know, do you think I should tell the police? The young man is a fugitive. The cops might be interested to know that he walked out of the Volkov residence and across to 3130 Dolphin Lane, where he knocked on the door and was invited inside."

"3130 Dolphin Lane?" echoed Beanie, recognizing the address. "Are you sure that's where Joshua went? To that house?"

A strange sense of unease snaked through Beanie.

3130 Dolphin Lane.

Why would Joshua go there? Beanie didn't understand, but he knew he could get the answer to his question.

"I am quite sure," said Mendez. "As I told you, my surveillance is top of the line, and—"

"Mr. Mendez, did Joshua leave that house?"

"I was just about to tell you," said Mendez. "I did an extensive search of my surveillance files, and I can say, without a doubt, that Joshua went into 3130 Dolphin Lane … but he didn't come out."

34

"I've been wanting to ask you about the Zeller case," said Old Wilson, leading Beanie through his home.

Beanie doubted the old man would feel that way when he revealed the reason for his visit. He'd shown up unannounced—taking a chance that the septuagenarian would be home—under the guise of needing a quote for a follow-up story about Dr. Zeller's attack.

After his conversation with Mendez, Beanie had viewed the surveillance video of Joshua leaving the Volkov house on October 29th, which Mendez had emailed him. Staring at his computer, Beanie watched with rapt anticipation, his pulse racing as Joshua walked out onto the Volkov's porch. After strolling down the driveway, he crossed the street and angled left, heading toward 3130 Dolphin Lane. The modest, shell-colored bungalow of Edgar Wilson.

Beanie glanced around, not surprised that the house was cloistered and cramped, crammed with too much furniture, most of it outdated and too large for the rooms it occupied. A cloying musty smell permeated the air. The atmosphere was humid and damp. Beanie felt a thin sheen of sweat breaking out on his back. He wondered if the old man was on a fixed income. Maybe trying to cut down on electricity costs by forgoing the A/C.

He followed Old Wilson down a short hall, navigating around several accent tables, a few indoor potted palm trees, and stepped over a crate filled with documents and files.

"We can talk in the kitchen," said Old Wilson, leading Beanie down the short hallway and into the small galley kitchen.

As Beanie took a seat at the round table, Old Wilson said, "I think Rufus Mason attacked the doctor."

"You do?" asked Beanie, keeping his tone neutral, non-accusatory. He was eager to confront the old man about Mendez's video of Joshua entering Old Wilson's house. Still, he had a feeling Old Wilson would become defensive and possibly combative if he felt under attack. Beanie wanted answers, but antagonizing the man might get him kicked out of the house.

Beanie's thoughts pivoted to his suspicions about Old Wilson.

On Joshua's podcast audio, he'd spoken about visiting the Fury follower, the old man who'd killed a woman. Not an old man who'd killed his wife, as Stevie had pointed out. An old man who most likely was not Rufus Mason, Beanie realized now. And if Mason wasn't the Fury follower, then who was the old man?

Old Wilson? Could that be right? Beanie wrestled with the theory, and the theory won. But how would he prove it? How could he prove that Old Wilson was the old man who'd killed a woman to impress the Fury?

Driving from the *Palmchat Gazette* offices to Oyster Farms, Beanie replayed Mendez's video over and over in his mind. The footage was startling and strange. Mendez swore there was no video of Joshua leaving Old Wilson's house, which Beanie found hard to believe, and yet couldn't deny. He couldn't help but think that there was no surveillance footage of Joshua leaving because the intern was still inside of Old Wilson's house. And no matter what, Beanie wasn't leaving until Old Wilson explained why Joshua had gone inside his house but had never left.

Even now, the thought sent a chill of apprehension and dread through Beanie.

Competing theories, both dire, plagued Beanie. If Joshua was still in Old Wilson's house, was it by choice? Or was the intern being held against his will?

Joshua had entered Old Wilson's house under his own volition. Willingly. No had forced him into the home. But if he hadn't left, was it because he'd wanted to stay? And, if so, what did that mean? Beanie fought panic. He knew what it meant, but he didn't want to believe it because it was too awful to be true. And he didn't want to confront the truth about Joshua. He didn't want Joshua to be a Fury follower. Didn't want the intern to have made a fool of him. Didn't want to consider the possibility that Joshua might be hiding in the house, listening, laughing to himself, waiting for a moment to impress the Fury by killing Beanie.

But what if Old Wilson was holding Joshua hostage? Maybe, as Beanie suspected, Joshua had gotten in over his head and had visited Old Wilson to inform him that he wasn't really a Fury follower and didn't want to kill anyone. Old Wilson could have become enraged. The old man might have felt duped. Manipulated. He might have knocked Joshua over the head and tied him up. Or, maybe he'd done something worse. Something Beanie didn't want to believe.

Beanie cleared his throat. "So, as I said, I'd like to get some quotes about what happened to Dr. Zeller from some of the residents on Dolphin Lane."

"You ask me, Mason is gonna get away with another murder," said Old Wilson, his eyes dancing with lurid excitement. "I know he attacked Dr. Zeller. The police need to do their jobs and find some evidence that will stick to that fiend, or we're all gonna end up under his Mango tree! You ask me, what they need to do is dig up the tree. I know they'll find Mason's wife in the dirt. Have you ever seen that tree? It's gorgeous, and I heard the mangos are the sweetest you ever tasted. Not that I have tried one myself, mind you, because I don't want to eat fruit from a tree fertilized with human remains."

Beanie said, "I'm not sure about that."

"Not sure about what?"

"About Rufus Mason killing his wife," said Beanie. "There's no proof. Just a rumor."

"Ain't no danged rumor," said Old Wilson. "Mason killed his wife because she was cheating on him."

"How do you know that?" asked Beanie.

Old Wilson scoffed. "Young man, I've lived in this house longer than you been alive. Me, Mason, and Mendez were some of the first residents of this community. On this street. I know all about Rufus and his wife, Althea. She was a loose woman. Fooled around with a lot of different men. She was very beautiful, and she knew it. That craven slut used her beauty against men."

"She did?" asked Beanie, staring at Old Wilson. The man scowled, his mouth twisted in a grim line, as though he tasted bile.

"You ask me," said Old Wilson, his gaze burning with something strange and manic. "Althea Mason got what she deserved."

Beanie frowned. "You think she deserved to die?"

Old Wilson blinked, as though becoming aware of something he hadn't expected. Clearing his throat, he said, "Anyway. If you don't have any more questions for me, then—"

"Actually, I did want to ask you about something else," said Beanie. "Joshua Howard."

Scowling, Old Wilson said, "Joshua Howard?"

"The student who was missing—"

"But he wasn't missing," snapped old Wilson.

"No, he wasn't," said Beanie.

Old Wilson's nostrils flared as his eyes narrowed. "So, why are you asking me about him?"

"I got a call earlier from Mr. Mendez," said Beanie. "He recently found footage of Joshua leaving the Volkov house."

Old Wilson blinked, then said, "You don't say. Well, what does it matter? The boy was never missing, and now he's on the run. A fugitive from justice. He's probably long gone, don't you think? Cops don't need to waste their time and our tax dollars looking for that boy."

"Well, it matters because Mendez's video shows Joshua leaving the Volkov's house, crossing the street, and then walking to your front door," said Beanie, deciding not to beat around the bush.

"My front door?" asked Old Wilson, his tone a mix of surprise and outrage. "That can't be right."

"In the surveillance footage, Joshua rings your doorbell, the door opens, and then he goes into the house, and the door closes," Beanie said. "I have a copy of the video on my phone, said Beanie. I can show it to you if—"

"Oh, you know what? Goodness me! My memory! Sometimes I worry

I'm suffering from dementia," said Old Wilson. "I do remember that the boy came to my house that night."

Beanie asked, "What did he want?"

"He was very upset," said Old Wilson. "He'd had an argument with the Volkovs about something, and the wife had lunged at him and tried to bite him. He was very terrified. So I told him to sit down and try to get himself together because he was angry. Spitting mad. He kept saying he wanted to kill the Volkovs for what they had done."

"What had they done?"

"He wouldn't say. Just kept saying he was going to kill Ivan Volkov," said Old Wilson. "Good Lord, I didn't take him seriously that night, but I suppose he made good on that threat."

"Did you tell the police?"

Old Wilson looked perplexed. "Tell them what?

"That you saw Joshua the night he disappeared," said Beanie. "That he came to your house and threatened to kill Volkov."

Old Wilson's eyes narrowed as he stared at Beanie. "I don't think I did."

"Why not?"

"Because I must not have remembered at the time," said Old Wilson, eyes flashing in defiance. "When the police spoke with me, I didn't think about it. Now, I'm sorry if you don't believe me, but—"

"No, I believe you," said Beanie, holding up his hands. "I was just wondering why you hadn't told the police, but if you didn't remember—"

"I know I should have remembered. I wish I had," said Old Wilson, his expression contrite. "I apologize for getting upset. When I say I am getting dementia, I am serious about that. I'm not just using the disease as an excuse for forgetfulness. It runs in my family."

Beanie asked, "So after Joshua threatened Volkov, what happened?"

"Well, I told him to leave," said Old Wilson. "His threats were making me very nervous, and he was so angry."

"And did he leave?"

Old Wilson stared at him for a moment, and then said, "He absolutely did."

"Did he say where he was going?"

"No, and I didn't ask," said Old Wilson. "I just wanted him gone, and I was glad when he went on his way. Thinking about that night, I'm thankful he didn't kill me."

"Why would Joshua kill you?" asked Beanie. "I thought you said he was angry at Ivan Volkov."

"Yes, that's true," said Old Wilson. "But, I had a Fury follower in my house that night."

Beanie's pulse jumped. "A Fury follower?"

"Joshua Howard is a Fury follower," said Old Wilson.

"Why do you think that?"

"It was in the article you wrote about him," said Old Wilson.

"I didn't write an article saying that Joshua is a Fury follower," said Beanie.

Old Wilson blinked. "Oh, well … hmmm, that's odd. I could have sworn that's what I read, but you know what, on second thought, I didn't read it. Friend of mine who works at the police station told me. I got my sources, too."

"You know, I think you should tell the police that Joshua came to your house after he left the Volkov's," said Beanie, a plan forming in his mind.

"What would be the point in doing that?" asked Old Wilson, eyes darting.

"The cops need to know that Joshua threatened Ivan Volkov," said Beanie. "And they'll probably want to look around your place."

"Look around my house?" Old Wilson said, voice raised, eyes wide. "For what?"

"Clues," said Beanie. "Joshua may have left something behind. Something that might help the police figure out where he went, or—"

"Oh my goodness, you are right," said Old Wilson.

"Right about what?" asked Beanie.

"I do have something that might help the police," said Old Wilson. "Something Joshua Howard left at my house."

Skeptical of the old man's claim, Beanie asked, "Joshua left something at your house?"

Nodding, Old Wilson said, "He absolutely did."

Beanie asked, "What did he leave?"

"A wallet," said Old Wilson, grunting as he rose to his feet. "Must have fallen out of his jacket. I was going to take it to the police station. It's out in my shed in the backyard. I have a safe out there where I keep important things."

"And you're sure it's Joshua's wallet?"

Old Wilson headed out of the kitchen. "Let me go and get it. Won't take me but two shakes of a lamb's tail."

Standing in the hallway just outside the galley kitchen, Beanie stared after the old man as he hurried down the hall toward the sunroom at the rear of the house. Through the glass patio doors, he surveyed the man's yard, a narrow rectangle, about fifteen to twenty yards long, dotted with a few young fruit trees. At the back of the yard, positioned next to the fence, was an old weather-beaten wooden shed.

Minutes later, Beanie saw the old man striding across the back yard toward the shed.

Beanie exhaled. He'd suggested that Old Wilson tell the police about his visit from Joshua to test the old man. If Old Wilson agreed to inform the authorities, Beanie would have been inclined to believe he was wrong about the man being the old Fury follower.

But, Old Wilson had balked at the idea.

The man's vehement reluctance was suspicious, but was it enough to confirm him as the Fury follower? The old man who confessed his obsession with a heinous serial killer. Beanie wasn't sure. Leaving the kitchen, he walked down the hall, heading for the sunroom.

Once again, he was in the position of having more gut instinct than proof. Was there any concrete evidence against Old Wilson? The man had seen Joshua on October 29th. But what else had he done? Wilson had argued with the Volkovs about packages on their porch. After Natalya bit Wilson, he'd denied putting packages on the Volkov porch, but what if he'd lied about that?

Continuing down the hall, Beanie passed the recessed dining nook. Something in his periphery caught his attention. Beanie glanced to the right, toward a square dining table positioned in the small area. On the wall behind the table was a striking piece of artwork. A large poster of a woman holding a hibiscus flower. A jolt shook Beanie. The poster was unflinchingly familiar. He'd seen it before.

Beanie's heart lurched.

When Joshua had called him, via Skype, the intern had sat at a table. Behind Joshua had been a large poster of a woman holding a hibiscus flower. Transfixed, Beanie stared at the poster.

The proof against Old Wilson was hanging on the dining room wall. Joshua hadn't left Old Wilson's house because the murdering old psychopath had kidnapped the intern. Joshua had seemed off during the video call. Now Beanie knew why. Old Wilson must have been out of sight of the camera, maybe holding a gun, forcing Joshua to pretend that he was okay.

Cursing under his breath, Beanie pulled out his cell phone and called Officer Fields. Minutes later, the Desk Sergeant told him Fields was out on a call. Frustrated, Beanie ended the call and then sent a quick text to Stevie. *Old Wilson is Fury follower. I'm with him now. Call cops. Old Wilson may have Joshua.* Beanie hurried toward the sunroom, anxious to confront Old Wilson, to demand that he tell him where Joshua was, and—

Ahead, through the glass doors of the sunroom, Beanie saw Old Wilson stumble out of the shed, clutching his chest. Beanie's pulse jumped. Was the old man having a heart attack, or—

Dropping to his knees, Old Wilson collapsed in the grass.

35

"Mr. Wilson?" Beanie ran toward the man, who lay face down in the grass and kneeled next to him. "Mr. Wilson? Are you okay? Can you hear me?"

Carefully, Beanie turned the old man over onto this back. What had happened? Beanie cursed. He'd taken a CPR course in college, but that was years ago, and he hadn't been recertified since, though he knew he needed to be, considering that he had two small children. He couldn't kick himself about it now. After checking Old Wilson's pulse, Beanie felt more relieved. Beneath his fingers, the beat was strong and steady. The man was still breathing, his chest rising and falling steadily, but he remained unconscious. The man appeared to be asleep. Old Wilson didn't look as though he was experiencing any medical distress, but Beanie couldn't take any chances. He needed to find his phone and call an ambulance.

Beanie reached into his pocket for his cell phone. It wasn't there. Confusion rocked him. Where was his phone? He'd just sent Stevie a text. Had he accidentally dropped it when he saw Wilson collapse?

"What … what happened?" groaned Old Wilson, eyelids fluttering.

"Mr. Wilson?" Beanie asked, helping the man sit up. "Mr. Wilson, are you hurt?"

"No, I'm not hurt," whispered Old Wilson, his eyes darting slowly as he glanced at Beanie. "I'm okay. Just a fainting spell."

"I'm going to call you an ambulance," said Beanie, hoping the man would agree with his suggestion. With Old Wilson at the hospital, he could look around the house for Joshua until the police arrived.

"No, no ambulance," said Old Wilson, waving a hand dismissively. "They cost a fortune, and anyway, there's nothing wrong with me."

Beanie said, "But I think—"

"I just fainted," said Old Wilson, traces of frustration and embarrassment in his gruff tone. "There's nothing wrong with me. I went into the shed, reached up to grab the string to turn on the light, and got dizzy, is all. Just need to take a few deep breaths and get my bearings."

"Are you sure?" asked Beanie.

Nodding, Old Wilson said, "I'll be fine, but I wasn't able to get the wallet out of the safe. I dropped the keys when I was inside the shed. Can you get them and open the safe for me?"

"Yeah, no problem," said Beanie, stepping into the shed. Peering into the darkness, he struggled to see. The sunshine made the interior of the shed appear darker. It was like looking into a cave. Waiting for his pupils to adjust the darkness, Beanie glanced down and—

A low moaning whispered around Beanie.

Beanie stood still, listening. The moaning grew louder, more insistent. Staring around the dark shed, Beanie discerned the faint outline of … what was that? At the back of the shed? Something was propped against the wall. Was that …? Someone sitting on the floor?

"Mr. Wilson?" Beanie called over his shoulder before he turned and—

Old Wilson, on his feet standing just outside the shed, gave Beanie a malevolent glare full of spite and rage before he slammed the door shut.

Beanie suffered a paralyzing panic as darkness enveloped him. Cursing, he tried to temper his frustration and anger. Old Wilson had tricked him. Lured him out to the backyard with some fake fainting spell so he could lock him in the shed.

Beanie ran to the door. Beating against the wood, Beanie grabbed the doorknob, yanking and turning it to no avail. He shuddered as an image of Old Wilson's face invaded his mind. Just before the man had locked him in the shed, Old Wilson's gaze was deranged, malicious evil dancing in his dark pupils.

Beanie forced himself to calm down. Taking a deep breath, he turned in a shaky circle. He couldn't see a thing. The shed was sealed tight. But Old Wilson had said he'd gotten dizzy while trying to turn on the light. Obviously, the man had lied about fainting. But had he lied about the light? Beanie hoped not. Figuring the string to activate the light would be toward the center of the shed, Beanie took a few cautious steps, and—

His foot brushed against something.

There was another moan.

A chill passed through Beanie as he remembered what he'd seen before Old Wilson had closed the door.

Someone propped against the back wall.

Spatially disoriented, he took a step back, stumbled, cried out, and unable to keep his balance, tumbled forward, landing on his hip. The moans intensified as Beanie rolled over and pushed himself up to a sitting position.

"Hello?" said Beanie. "Is someone in here?"

His answer was a grunting moan, more pronounced, as though whoever was in the shed was trying to speak but couldn't.

"Is there a gag around your mouth?" guessed Beanie.

More grunting, seemingly in the affirmative.

"Are you tied up?"

Again, grunts that sounded as though the person was trying to say yes.

"Okay, I'm going to stand up and try to turn on the light," said Beanie, making his way to his feet. On shaky legs, he wobbled slightly. Steadying himself, Beanie lifted his arm and waved his hand around. Something slid against his thumb, and he caught hold of it. Grasping the thin rope, he yanked it down. Weak light illuminated the shed, brightening the dark corners and crevices, revealing bare wooden walls. The shed was empty.

Moans and grunts, behind Beanie, arrested his attention.

He turned. "What the…?"

36

Beanie stared into the wide, furtive eyes staring back at him.

Familiarity and realization struck simultaneously as he took in the pale, blotchy face, matted russet-red hair, and patchy beard clinging to the jaw and chin. Despite the cuts, scratches, and bruises on the skin, Beanie recognized the guy huddled on the floor in the corner, bound and gagged.

What he didn't recognize was the person in the opposite corner, which appeared to be a man curled in the fetal position, unconscious.

"Joshua?" Thankful to see the intern alive, Beanie stared at him. Joshua looked like a prisoner of war. Like he'd been captured behind enemy lines. He was banged up, dirty, and he smelled.

Joshua's head bobbed up and down as he grunted and groaned words muffled by the strips of cloth wrapped several times around his mouth. Hurrying to the student, Beanie maneuvered behind him, untied the rags, and yanked them down until they hung around Joshua's throat like a cloth necklace.

"We gotta get out of here!" croaked Joshua, his voice hoarse. "Wilson is gonna kill us, and he's probably gonna kill you! He locked both of us in here!"

Beanie glanced at the unmoving form. "Both of you?"

"Me and Rufus Mason!"

His heart kicking, Beanie stared at the unconscious man as he maneuvered behind Joshua. Dropping to one knee, he said, "Tell me what happened."

Joshua said, "Edgar Wilson is a Fury follower—"

"I know that part," said Beanie. "Tell me how he locked you in here."

"The Friday before Halloween, I went to the Volkovs to warn them that Wilson wanted to kill Ivan," began Joshua. "But Ivan wasn't home. Only the wife was there, and I didn't really want to be alone with her and didn't think I should considering that my lawsuit against her was still pending."

Wrestling with the thick rope wound around Joshua's wrists, Beanie asked, "What did she say when you told her that Wilson was going to kill her husband?"

"I don't even know if she understood me," said Joshua. "She got really agitated and started speaking Russian, so I decided to leave before she lunged at me again. Then I went to Wilson's."

"Why?" asked Beanie, yanking on the rope, trying to loosen it.

"I wanted to trick the old fart," said Joshua. "Wanted to get a recording of Wilson admitting that he planned to kill Ivan Volkov. Once he got permission from the Fury, of course. That's why Wilson was writing letters to the Fury. Which was so dumb. Like the prison was even going to let the Fury read that crap. The only thing they allow the Fury to read is the Bible, and that's after someone has gone through every page to make sure there are no secret messages hidden in the Scriptures. I found all that out when I was researching the Fury for my paper."

"Did you tell Wilson that?"

"I tried, but he didn't believe me," said Joshua. "Anyway, I was gonna take the recording to the cops. But, Wilson tricked me, instead."

"He faked a fainting spell?" guessed Beanie.

"How'd you know?" asked Joshua.

"Why do you think I'm locked in here with you?"

Scoffing, Joshua said, "I thought he'd had a heart attack. I was about to call an ambulance when Wilson knocked me out. I woke up in the shed, bound and gagged. Don't even know how long I've been here. Can't believe the old fart bothered to feed me."

"But Wilson allowed you to make the Skype call with me?"

"Wilson didn't want anyone looking for me," said Joshua. "When you wrote those articles about me possibly being missing, Wilson freaked out. During that Skype call, he had a gun on me. He was standing a few feet away, out of sight of the laptop camera. Before the call, Wilson told me if I screamed or tried to send a coded message, he would blow my head off."

"And what about your finger?"

"That evil old fool bit it off when I tried to escape. It was the day before Halloween. He wanted me to send a text to some of my friends, but he couldn't figure out how to use my phone. He had to untie me, and as soon as he loosened the ropes, I took my chance. We wrestled for a good while. He's not as frail as he looks. Couldn't believe he bit my finger off."

"Did he bandage it up?"

Nodding, Joshua said, "He stitched me up. Did a pretty good job, actually. Gave me antibiotics and a sedative. I slept for a few days, then woke up in the shed again."

A sputtering cough, followed by a low moan made Beanie jump. He glanced toward Mason, who had rolled onto his back, revealing that he, too, had been bound with thick rope.

"Mr. Mason, are you okay?" Beanie rushed to the older man and helped him to a sitting position. "It's Roland Bean—"

"I know who you are," gasped Mason, leaning his head back against the wall. "That old degenerate didn't blindfold me. I can see fine. He just tied me up."

The man's craggy, skeletal face was bruised. Judging from the yellow-greenish color of the wounds around his right eye and near his left chin, Beanie guessed Mason had been in the shed a few days.

"What happened?" Beanie asked Mason. "How did you get in here?"

"They say no good deed goes unpunished," wheezed Mason.

"What do you mean?" asked Beanie.

Joshua said, "He was trying to rescue me."

"You knew Joshua was in Wilson's shed?"

His head bobbing slowly, Mason said, "Few nights before Halloween, I was on my front porch enjoying the night sky when I saw Joshua walk from the Volkov's place to Wilson's house. I saw Joshua enter Wilson's house, but

I didn't see Joshua leave. I sat on my porch all night, but Joshua didn't come out."

"Because Wilson had knocked me out," said Joshua.

"I had no knowledge of that at the time," said Mason. "But I was suspicious. And when I read the article about Joshua being missing and saw his photo online, I remembered the red hair. I had a feeling Wilson had harmed the young man. So, I kept watching Wilson's house. One afternoon, while at the market, I saw Mrs. March, who is Wilson's next-door neighbor. She complained that Wilson was keeping her up going in and out of his shed after midnight."

"He was bringing me bread and water," said Joshua.

Mason said, "My suspicions grew. One night, I decided to pay Wilson a visit under the guise of discussing the wolf sightings. Wilson made coffee, and we drank as we talked. I don't much care for coffee, but Wilson had several cups and soon had to relieve himself. While he was in the bathroom, I went out into the backyard to the shed and knocked on the door."

"I was gagged, but when I heard the knocking, I knew it couldn't be Wilson," said Joshua. "He would never knock. So, I tried to scream around the gag."

"I heard the muffled cries," said Mason. "I tried to open the door, but it was locked. Knowing that Wilson had someone held hostage in the shed, I took out my phone and ..."

"And ...what?" asked Beanie, riveted by the account.

Mason sighed. "And that's the last thing I remember. Wilson must have clocked me."

"The door opened, and I thought I was saved," said Joshua. "But no. Wilson dragged Mason into the shed, tied him up, and left us both in here."

Unnerved by Mason's story, Beanie went back to Joshua and began working to untie the knots. Minutes later, he yanked one last time, and the rope, unknotted, dropped to the floor.

"Thank God!" exclaimed Howard, carefully touching his abraded wrists. "Thought I would never be free. Thought I was going to die in this shed, and for what? Stupid podcast that no one would even listen to."

Beanie begged to differ, but he said, "Unfortunately, you're not free yet. None of us are. We're all still locked in this shed."

"Hey, you smell that?" Mason asked.

Beanie tensed. "What?"

"Smells like …" Joshua sniffed.

Mason asked, "Is that gasoline?"

Panic flooded Beanie as he inhaled. The unmistakable pungent smell of gas floated into the air.

"Why would we be smelling gas?" asked Joshua, fear overwhelming his features.

Beanie swallowed. "I don't know … is there a gas can in here?"

"There's nothing in here," said Joshua.

Glancing around, Beanie knew he would find the shed empty. He'd already determined that when he'd turned on the light and—

"The shed is on fire!" screamed Joshua, pointing toward the ceiling.

Beanie looked up.

His heart sank when he saw the orange flames.

37

"We gotta get out of here!" shouted Joshua, scrambling to his feet.

Mason struggled to stand. "Wilson's going to burn us alive!"

As thick, dark smoke filled the small shed, Beanie's heart slammed. Fighting panic, he looked around the shed. Above them, flames licked the roof. Beanie's gaze followed the fire as it snaked down the side of the shed wall, crackling and devouring the wooden planks. Smoke invaded his nose and mouth. He coughed as heat wafted across his skin.

Beanie tried to focus, but all he could think was that Joshua was right.

Old Wilson was trying to burn them alive. The thought of burning to death consumed his mind. Fear gripped him as he contemplated never seeing his kids again. He couldn't fathom the idea of not being there to watch them grow up. Becoming sullen teenagers. Going to college. Turning into young men with their own families.

Several planks of burning plywood crashed down from the roof.

Cursing, Beanie grabbed Joshua and pulled him toward the corner of the shed that wasn't on fire.

"We can't just stand here and die!" Joshua said. "We gotta do something!"

Across from him, the wall of fire popped and spewed flames.

Forcing himself to ignore the dire direction of his thoughts, Beanie nodded and looked up. Above him, through the jagged hole in the roof caused by the falling plywood, the powder blue sky mesmerized Beanie. Would he ever feel the hot St. Killian sun on his face again? Or the balmy, humid sea breeze against his skin?

"We gotta get out through the roof," said Beanie. "That's our best chance. Maybe our only chance ..."

Coughing, Mason said, "Roof looks to be about two feet above us."

Beanie glanced up, then looked at Joshua. "Think you can climb through the hole?"

Joshua looked uncertain. "I don't know!"

Beanie said, "I'll lift you up and then you can—"

Flames exploded and burst from the wall.

"What about the fire?" asked Joshua, his voice hoarse with panic.

Staring at the flames dancing around the rim of the hole in the roof, Beanie said, "I'll lift you straight up through the hole!"

"And then what?" asked Joshua, his eyes darting, hints of suppressed panic in his tone.

Coughing, Mason said, "You can crawl out on top of the roof, then jump down and open the door for us!"

Oppressive heat nearly smothered Beanie as smoke swirled through the air, clouding the shed, making it nearly impossible to see.

"Are you sure that will work?" Joshua shook his head. "What if—"

"We have to try!" Mason insisted. "We don't have a choice!"

Worried that Joshua would be burned, Beanie yelled, "I'll give you my shirt! You can wrap it around your head!"

Hesitating, Joshua shook his head. "I don't know if—"

A sizzling splutter of flames rained down beside them as more planks dropped from the roof.

"Come on. We have to hurry!" Beanie shouted, removing his short-sleeved button-down. Fingers trembling, he took in the stained and torn T-shirt and grimy khaki shorts Joshua wore. Could his plan work? Or would the student be horrifically burned as he tried to scramble across the flaming, crumbling roof?

Beanie expelled a barking, hoarse cough as searing, sweltering heat threatened to suffocate him. He tossed his shirt toward Joshua. "Hurry! Wrap it around your head!"

"We're running out of time!" Mason yelled. "We can't—"

Soapy, wet foam, and water rained down on Beanie, drenching him as his mind reeled. More water splashed down, extinguishing the hissing, sizzling flames.

Loud thudding slammed against the structure. Disoriented, his heart punching against his chest, Beanie stumbled back as splinters of wood flew toward him, mixing with the foamy water.

Piercing lasers of bright light shot through the broken wood as the door began to split and break apart. Moments later, gloved hands reached through the shed door and pulled it open. Shouting and crying, Joshua rushed to the door. Coughing and cupping a hand above his eyes, Beanie peered through the swirling smoke. Several firefighters grabbed Joshua and helped him out of the shed. Legs trembling, Beanie lumbered to the door.

"Easy, easy," cautioned one of the firemen. "We got you."

Assisted by the first responders, Beanie gulped breaths of fresh air as he stumbled out into the hazy sunshine of a balmy St. Killian afternoon. Quickly surrounded by cops and EMS responders swarming the backyard, Beanie collapsed in the grass.

EPILOGUE

Wilson had planned to burn them alive, thought Beanie, staring at the ceiling above the bed where he'd been resting for the past few hours, in his room at St. Killian General Hospital.

Squeezing his eyes shut, Beanie struggled to control his anger.

Everything he'd thought he'd known about Edgar Wilson was a lie.

A Fury follower had lived on Dolphin Lane for decades. An evil old deceiver who'd committed a heinous crime. A twisted fiend who'd fooled everyone into thinking he was just a nosey old busybody with an overactive imagination, a lonely man with too much time on his hands. Wilson had exploited those misguided judgments. The old man had allowed people to think he was a half-senile busybody, and all the while, he'd hid a dark, sinister past.

Beanie coughed. He felt blessed that he, Joshua, and Rufus Mason had only suffered mild smoke inhalation. Things could have been worse, he knew.

His wife could have lost her husband. His kids could have lost their father. Beanie hated thinking of the trauma his family would have experienced, learning of the horrific way he would have died. He prayed that if he'd had to die like that, then Noelle would have spared the boys any gruesome details.

He was thankful Stevie had received his text and called the cops. Grateful that one of Old Wilson's neighbors had seen the shed in flames and called the fire department. More than anything, Beanie had been relieved to learn Old Wilson had been captured and put in jail.

The police had found the old man hiding in his attic. Initially, during his interrogation, Old Wilson feigned ignorance, claiming he had no idea that Joshua, Rufus Mason, and Beanie had been locked in his shed. He claimed he hadn't used the shed in years and that Joshua and Mason must have been squatting in the dwelling without his knowledge. When confronted with evidence of chloroform, rope, a Taser, and several guns found in his home, Old Wilson changed his story. Joshua and Mason, both Fury followers, had tried to kill him, so he'd knocked the men out and locked them in the shed. As for how Beanie had ended up in the shed, Old Wilson claimed not to know.

Wilson had denied killing Ivan Volkov, even though some of the man's possessions—Volkov's wallet, company ID badge, and car keys—had been found in his home. The cops located bloody articles of Volkov's clothing in the closet of a guest bedroom, but Wilson insisted he had no idea how they'd gotten there.

As for murdering Rufus Mason's wife, Althea, and writing letters to the Fury, Old Wilson insisted it was all a heinous plot orchestrated by Mason to frame him and besmirch his good name.

Indignation and anger seized Beanie when he considered Old Wilson's diabolical delusion. The old man was a homicidal maniac who didn't seem to think he'd done anything wrong. Did the lying murderer believe that if he denied the charges against him, then they weren't true?

There was a knock at the door.

Exhaling, Beanie called out, "Come in ..."

Moments later, Joshua entered the room, dressed in a hospital gown. Pulling an IV pole, he gave Beanie a sheepish smile. "You mind a visitor?"

"Not at all," said Beanie, smiling. "Take a seat."

As Joshua settled himself in the chair across from the bed, Beanie asked, "How are you?"

"I'll live," said the intern. "Thanks to you. That's why I'm here. Don't think I thanked you for saving my life."

"No need to thank me," said Beanie. "I was happy to do it."

Nodding, Joshua looked away for a moment, and Beanie guessed that the intern was struggling to process the gravity of what they'd suffered, what they'd been blessed to survive. Things could have ended so differently, so devastatingly. Reflecting on what they'd survived was something Beanie knew they would continue to do.

Clearing his throat, Joshua said, "So, there's something I was wondering and figured I'd just ask."

"What's that?"

"How did you know I was trapped in the shed?"

Beanie sighed. "I didn't know until I was trapped in there with you and Mason. I'd gone to Old Wilson's because I suspected he was the Fury follower you'd talked about in your podcast audio notes."

Joshua nodded. "Friday told me she gave you the stuff in my duffel bag. Thank God she did. By the way, we're not broken up. Wilson forced me to dump her, so she'd stop looking for me."

Beanie said, "Friday is an interesting young lady, but she cares about you."

"She's kinda different." Joshua chuckled. "But, so am I. So, we're good for each other."

Nodding, Beanie said, "Hey, there's something I was wondering ... in your podcast, you said you found out that Old Wilson was sending the letters to the Fury, not the Volkovs. How?"

"I got a friend in the Island Parcel accounting department to research who paid for the packages to Tiverton," said Joshua. "I did that because I was trying to prove that the Volkovs were Fury followers, which, as you know, was what I initially thought."

"And you wanted to prove they were Fury followers because you wanted leverage to use against them in your lawsuit," said Beanie.

Pink splotches colored Joshua's cheeks as he looked down. "Not something I'm proud of, but I was listening to my lawyer. Which I shouldn't have. Shouldn't have even filed the lawsuit."

"That stuff in your notebook about taking down Volkov," began Beanie. "Was that your lawyer's idea?"

Joshua nodded. "After the mediation went nowhere, my lawyer

suggested I get dirt on the Volkovs. When I picked up that package to the Fury from their porch, I thought I had the dirt I needed."

"But the Volkovs had no idea what you were talking about," said Beanie.

"That's why I wanted to prove that they were sending the packages to the Fury," said Joshua. "Instead, I found out the packages were being paid for by Edgar Wilson."

"And when you found that out, you decided to approach him about your podcast," said Beanie.

Joshua said, "Probably wasn't the best idea …

"Actually, as dangerous as it was, you were doing some good undercover investigative journalism," said Beanie. "Lots of atrocities have been exposed by brave reporters willing to risk their lives to get the story."

"Yeah, a story that almost got me killed," grumbled Joshua. "Wasn't thinking that at the time, though. I was thinking how cool it would be to get an actual Fury follower for my podcast, so I decided to trick him. Decided I would introduce myself as someone who had something in common with him."

"You pretended to be a Fury follower?"

"I figured that was my best chance to get him to talk to me. For a while, it was working," said Joshua. "He was telling me all this stuff about the Fury. He told me he'd sinned against the Fury."

"Sinned against him, how?"

"Twenty years ago," said Joshua, "Wilson pissed the Fury off. Apparently, Wilson and the Fury shared the same lover. A woman named Althea Mason."

"Rufus Mason's wife?"

Joshua nodded. "Right. Althea Mason was a secret Fury follower. She lured lots of tourists, mostly men, because she was supposedly smoking hot back in the day, to caves where the Fury was waiting to kill them. Anyway, she was having affairs with the Fury and with Wilson, which enraged Wilson. So, Wilson killed Althea, cut her up, and buried her beneath the mango tree in Mason's backyard."

"Wow …" Beanie said, recalling the venomous judgment Old Wilson had spewed against Mason's wife. He'd called her a loose woman. Said she'd deserved what happened to her. What he'd done to her.

"The Fury was furious—pardon the pun—when he found out that Wilson had killed Althea," said Joshua. "Not so much because he was in love with Althea, but because she brought him lots of victims. So, the Fury excommunicated Wilson from his group of followers. For decades, Wilson has been looking for a way to be welcomed back by the Fury. He keeps writing these letters begging the Fury for forgiveness. He told me he needed to give the Fury a sacrifice to get back in the serial killer's good graces."

"A sacrifice?"

"Wilson had to kill somebody," said Joshua.

"And he decided to kill Ivan Volkov," said Beanie.

"Actually, he was going to kill me," said Joshua. "Wilson killed Volkov because Volkov had confronted Wilson about putting packages on the Volkov's porch. Volkov had opened a few of the letters and knew that Wilson was a Fury follower. One of the letters talked about Wilson getting rid of Althea Mason and burying her under the mango tree. Volkov was going to show the letters to the PIIB."

Beanie exhaled. "So, Wilson had to kill Volkov."

His expression anguished, Joshua said, "I tried to stop it from happening, but maybe I didn't try hard enough."

"You can't blame yourself," said Beanie. "Old Wilson is a psycho. He tried to kill all of us."

Shaking his head, Joshua said, "Maybe if I had gone to the cops as soon as Wilson told me he wanted to kill Ivan Volkov ..."

"Why didn't you?"

"I didn't think they would believe me unless I had proof," said Joshua. "I kept trying to get him on tape, but he's a sly old psychopath. Every time I brought up killing Ivan Volkov, he didn't want to talk about it. I think he was suspicious of me. So then I thought I could stop Wilson by warning Volkov."

"But he wasn't there that night," said Beanie.

Joshua exhaled. "When I woke up in the shed after Wilson knocked me out, I knew he would kill Volkov, and there would be nothing I could do about it. I prayed that I would be wrong, but then ... "

"Then ...?" prompted Beanie, worried by the torment in the intern's apprehensive gaze.

"One night, the shed door opened," said Joshua. "I expected Wilson to throw in a few pieces of bread and a bottle of water. When he fed me, he would come in and shoot me with a Taser. Then he'd untie me, and after I stopped shaking, he would hold a gun on me while I ate the bread and drank the water."

"That's terrible."

"Anyway, that night, there was no bread or water. Wilson dragged a body into the shed. Volkov's dead body. Wilson had stabbed him to death. Volkov accused him of putting a package to the Fury on Volkov's porch. That's how Wilson would send the packages. He didn't want them picked up from his house, so he took them to Volkov's house, usually when Volkov was at work."

"But Volkov's body was found in the jungle," said Beanie.

"Wilson stored the body in the shed for a few days," said Joshua. "He made me stay in this shed with a dead man. I barely slept. Then one afternoon, I woke up, and Volkov's body was gone."

"And you know that Wilson tried to make it look like you killed Volkov," said Beanie.

"He forced me to grab the hilt of the knife he used to kill Volkov," said Joshua.

"Did you know he tried to frame Mason as well?" asked Beanie. "He tried to make it look like Mason tried to kill Dr. Zeller. He stole Mason's credit card and charged a plane ticket to Spain. He was trying to make it look as though Mason had fled the island. He also put Dr. Zeller's blood on one of Mason's shirts and hid the bloody shirt in Mason's washing machine."

"I'm not surprised," said Joshua. "Wilson hated Dr. Zeller. He told me that Zeller caught him placing packages on the Volkovs porch after he'd killed Ivan. Zeller intercepted the packages and saw they were addressed to the Fury. He read the letter and realized that Wilson was a Fury follower. Zeller confronted Wilson, but the old man denied sending the packages."

Beanie said, "Dr. Zeller called me the day he was attacked. He asked me to meet him because he wanted to discuss Rufus Mason. Of course, by the time I arrived at Zeller's home, Wilson had already nearly stabbed him to death. I'm pretty sure Dr. Zeller wanted to tell me that Mason wasn't the Fury follower and had nothing to do with Ivan's murder."

"What a crazy story, huh?" asked Joshua, shaking his head.

"A crazy story that you need to tell," said Beanie.

Joshua stared at him. "Huh?"

"Once I get out of here," said Beanie. "I'm going to talk to Vivian about you writing the story of how Wilson tried to kill us."

"Are you serious?" asked Joshua. "I thought you would write it."

Beanie laughed softly. "I've had enough of writing stories about situations and circumstances that I've been involved in."

"But that's part of your brand," said Joshua. "You write stories that you're part of."

"Yeah, I know," said Beanie. "But this is not my story. It's yours. You have a unique point of view. Trust me, if you tell this story, you'll probably end up on Sky News or Good Morning Britain or Caribbean Life."

Joshua's eyes widened. "You think so?"

"It's possible," said Beanie. "So, are you ready to tell the world how you met the man who followed the monster to hell and back?"

Did you figure out who the severed finger belonged to?

There were a lot of suspects and even more sinister secrets to uncover but once Beanie figured out all the deadly motives, he discovered the killer.

Halloween brought a corpse in the jungle and rumors of a spooky shapeshifter.

Thanksgiving, that time where we all give thanks for bountiful blessings, brings more mayhem when a man is poisoned at a Turkey Day backyard party ... or, is he?

In *Gobble Gobble Murder*, you'll have to figure out ...

Was a Thanksgiving party host accidentally poisoned? Or was he murdered?

Investigative reporter Roland "Beanie" Bean attends a Thanksgiving party where the host seems to suffer an allergic reaction. Soon, the police reveal the man was poisoned, but how? And who killed him? His cheating wife? His bitter ex-wife? Or a mysterious stranger who'd been sending him bizarre threats? Assigned to cover the case, Beanie is determined to uncover the truth, but discovering the murderer will force him to face a ruthless killer determined to make sure the truth stays hidden.

Gobble Gobble Murder is a holiday cozy murder mystery novel with plenty of twists and turns to keep you guessing until the shocking ending!

Get your copy of Gobble Gobble Murder now!

Are you eagerly anticipating Beanie's next unexpected detour into a mystery waiting to be solved?

Then **Beanie's Mini Mystery Moments** are for you!

Get an exclusive quick-read mystery that spins off from one of Beanie's mystery adventures delivered straight to your email inbox!
https://BookHip.com/ZMCRMGD

ALSO BY RACHEL WOODS

SASSY SARCASTIC CAT COZY MYSTERIES

Sophie Carter, a struggling reporter for the *Palmchat Gazette*, teams up with a sassy talking Calico cat to solve crimes as she strives to become an influential investigative reporter

A SLY AND SINISTER TAIL

A COLD AND CALCULATING TAIL

A FOUL AND FRIGHTENING TAIL

A DARK AND DEVIOUS TAIL

REPORTER ROLAND BEAN COZY MYSTERIES

Roland "Beanie" Bean, husband and loving father, finds himself the unwitting participant in solving crimes as he seeks to make a name for himself as a reporter for the *Palmchat Gazette.*

HAPPY BIRTHDAY MURDER

EASTER EGG HUNT MURDER

MERRY CHRISTMAS MURDER

TRICK OR TREAT MURDER

GOBBLE GOBBLE MURDER

HAPPY 4TH OF JULY MURDER

SUMMER VACATION MURDER

HAPPY NEW YEAR MURDER

PALMCHAT ISLANDS MYSTERIES

Married journalists, Vivian and Leo, manage the island newspaper while solving crimes as they chase leads for their next story.

UNTIL DEATH DO US PART

NO ONE WILL FIND YOU

YOU WILL DIE FOR THIS

DON'T MAKE ME HURT YOU

THE PALMCHAT ISLANDS MYSTERIES BOX SET: BOOKS 1 - 4

RUTHLESS REVENGE ROMANCE SERIES

Gripping romantic suspense series with steamy romance, unpredictable plot twists and devastating consequences of deceit.

HER DEADLY MISTAKE

HER DEADLY DECEPTION

HER DEADLY THREAT

HER DEADLY BETRAYAL

MURDER IN PARADISE SERIES

A series of stand-alone women sleuth mysteries with murder, mayhem and a dash of romance, set against the backdrop of turquoise waters and swaying palm trees of the fictional Palmchat Islands.

THE UNWORTHY WIFE

THE SILENT ENEMY

THE PERFECT LIAR

ABOUT THE AUTHOR

Rachel Woods studied journalism and graduated from the University of Houston where she published articles in the Daily Cougar. She is a legal assistant by day and a freelance writer and blogger with a penchant for melodrama by night. Many of her stories take place on the islands, which she has visited around the world. Rachel resides in Houston, Texas with her three sock monkeys.

For more information:
www.therachelwoods.com
rachel@therachelwoods.com

ABOUT THE PUBLISHER

BONZAIMOON BOOKS

BonzaiMoon Books is a family-run, artisanal publishing company created in the summer of 2014. We publish works of fiction in various genres. Our passion and focus is working with authors who write the books you want to read, and giving those authors the opportunity to have more direct input in the publishing of their work.

For more information:
www.bonzaimoonbooks.com
info@bonzaimoonbooks.com

9 781943 685486